Winged Life

WINGED LIFE

Hannah Hurnard

Tyndale House Publishers, Inc.
Wheaton, Illinois

Twelfth printing, November 1986

Library of Congress Catalog Card Number 78-54037
ISBN 0-8423-8225-9, paper
United States publications rights
secured by Tyndale House Publishers, Inc.,
Wheaton, Illinois 60187.
Published with the permission of
The Church's Ministry Among the Jews (Olive Press),
London, England.
American edition copyright © 1978 by
Tyndale House Publishers, Inc.
Reset and reissued, May 1979
Printed in the United States of America

Contents

CHAPTER 1
Winged Life

"They that wait upon the Lord shall renew their strength; they shall mount up with wings as eagles" (Isa. 40:31).

"God who is rich in mercy, for his great love wherewith he loved us... hath quickened us together with Christ... and hath raised us up together and made us sit together in heavenly places in Christ Jesus" (Eph. 2:4-6).

Some time ago when I was visiting the Cheddar Gorge I clambered up a steep hill of piled up rocks, and seating myself upon the topmost one, looked up at the strange pinnacled cliffs towering above me in every direction. Perched up there, high above the winding road, I noticed that the cliffs were riddled with holes and that multitudes of birds were entering and leaving the holes which, apparently, they used as nesting places. I realized that the cliffs formed an impregnable rock city for the birds, who were swooping to their nests, then coming out again and launching themselves on the air and wheeling about in loveliest freedom. They seemed so tantalizingly unearthbound as they soared jubilantly in the sky, exulting in their wings and filling the gorge with their songs.

As I watched them it broke upon my mind with a shock of delight and illumination that the birds really are a most perfect picture of the life in the heavenly places to which our Lord and Savior calls his followers. We see in them a perfect illustration of the life which every Christian is entitled to live here and now; risen with Christ, in the world but not of it.

Studying the birds wheeling about in the boundless sky, their wings seemed to spell out this lovely message of a higher life, up on a higher plane, obeying higher laws and possessing higher powers than ordinary human beings know anything about. The winged life of the heavenly places!

When the Lord Jesus came into the world

preaching the kingdom of heaven surely he was challenging men to allow him to lift them up to a higher form of life altogether, as different as is a bird's life from that of a mole burrowing in the ground. Then why do so many of us who really are his followers remain so drearily earthbound and so obviously unable to feel at home in the heavenly places? Indeed, many of us for years seem to have no wings at all by which to mount up into that life of glorious liberty.

We are terribly conscious of lack of joy, lack of power, lack of victory and lack of love. Worse still, we so often experience depression, moodiness, boredom, frustration, fear of being alone and at the same time inability to get along with our fellow workers and even with the members of our own families.

We are slaves to wrong habits, are unable to master our impulses and instincts, suffer from ugly deformities of character and are in complete bondage to our own difficult temperaments. We get so depressed with ourselves, above all, by our strange inability to obey the one commandment of our Lord to love one another. And because we find ourselves so unable to face up to the testings and temptations of life in a triumphant way, or to bear the strain of difficult circumstances, sometimes a nervous breakdown is the result.

Why is it that so few Christians know in actual experience what it is to enjoy the winged life of the heavenly places? Is it not because we know so little about love? Love is the law of the winged life. Up there in the heavenly places is to be experienced the perfect freedom and joy of those who have learned to love truly and have received power to do so continually and under all circumstances.

"If the Son shall make you free," said the Lord of the high places to all his earthbound and self-enslaved hearers, "ye shall be free indeed" (John 8:36). "Only love!" cried his servant St. Augustine. "Only obey the law of love and then do as you like."

There are three lovely characteristics about the life of a bird which distinguish it from the life of all earthbound creatures who do not possess wings. And the same things are characteristic of the heavenly places.

First, the birds can mount up into another region altogether and can soar beyond the reach of their enemies and all the snares laid for them on the earth beneath. They are absolutely free, and as long as they remain up there in the sky no one can set any limits to their freedom nor lay any restraints upon them.

Second, they can see much more and much farther than can other creatures walking on the earth. Theirs is a sphere of lovely vision and far distances. The higher they go, the further they can see. And how true it is that they who love most, see most.

Love opens the eyes of our understanding and enables us to see more of the truth than can those who are blinded by self-love. As I sat there in the Cheddar Gorge with the cliffs walling me in on every side, I could see no distance at all; but the birds wheeling overhead, high above the crags which blocked my view, could see the whole fair landscape spread out below them, far and wide in every direction.

Third, there is the song life of the birds and also of those who live in the heavenly places; the joy of those who sing out of triumphant experience, "Our soul is escaped as a bird out of the snare of the fowlers: the snare is broken and we are escaped" (Psa. 124:7). And again, "Though ye have lien among the pots, yet shall ye be as the wings of a dove covered with silver, and her feathers with yellow gold" (Psa. 68:13).

For many years of my Christian life I longed to know the secret of the winged life and to be able to live in the heavenly places far above all the power and might of our great enemy; able to live an overcoming life in touch with new powers and new energies which would enable me to do things which hitherto had seemed impossible or which could only be achieved with great strain and difficulty. At last, when the time was fully come, the lovely experience began to come true! Our Lord showed me the secret of being able to mount up on wings little by little (like young birds learning to fly) through the complete transformation of my thought life; and by learning radiant new lessons in love.

In this book I have tried to share what may perhaps be best described as "First Lessons in the Winged Life." And also, at the same time, to describe some of the wonderful new things which have broken in on my own understanding as a result of being able to look at things from the winged point of view, as it were, while taking short flights from tree to tree, and up to the top of the cliffs! Such radiant things! And so gloriously far-reaching that they really cannot be described. But oh, how they make me long to soar higher on the wings of love and to see more!

Perhaps through this book, some who have not yet begun the winged life, will know and feel that the time has come for them to begin it too, and will hear their Lord calling to them to come up to the high places, where all the loveliest songs are sung.

CHAPTER 2
Operation Broken Bottles

"Men do not put new wine into old skin bottles, lest the bottles break and the wine runneth out and the bottles perish. But they put new wine into new bottles, and both are preserved" (Matt. 9:17).

Once upon a time, when I was traveling in the West Indies, I stayed as a guest on one of the mission compounds, and there I came upon a book by a writer who has often greatly helped me. It was *The Garden of the Soul*, by Mrs. Herman, and one phrase in that book seemed to fit into my understanding like a golden key, offering me a clue to a particular phase of experience, very strange and bewildering, through which I had been passing for several years.

"The true meaning of words is only learned in the school of affliction."

In the same paragraph and on the same page was a quotation from Carlyle: "All thought worth thinking is conceived in the furnace of suffering."

These sentences seemed to illumine my mind very much in the same way as a flash of lightning suddenly rends the veil of darkness and reveals a whole landscape hitherto hidden and unsuspected. In the flash of insight and understanding which broke upon me then, I glimpsed the fact that vast and lovely realms of truth are spread out all around us. These realms of truth are waiting to be entered and explored with joy by those who are ready and willing to be shown fuller and richer meanings to many words and sayings in the Scriptures, which they have been too dull and too blind to see until the Lord lovingly leads them into the school of affliction and sorrow.

How true it is! and yet how extraordinarily slow some of us are to grasp it, that the true meaning of words, especially of the words in the Bible, can only be learned as we pass through life's varying experiences of bereavement, pain, loss, frustration, disappointment and heartbreak. Sorrow seems able to put into our hands a golden key which can unlock to us treasuries of truth and new understanding, far more often and more fully than joy can do.

When I was a young student at Bible school I never so much as suspected this fact, but was happily certain that I was there on purpose to learn from competent teachers the exact and true meaning of everything written in the inspired Scriptures. "There is only one truth," I told myself confidently, "and everything not in harmony with the one true interpretation is wholly false. I am fortunate and privileged to be learning from those who know the truth and will not lead me into error."

It never occurred to me that all that the greatest Christian teachers can do is to make us familiar with the signposts of the Scriptures by way of which the Holy Spirit himself will lead us on into the vast and glorious realms of truth and open up those realms to us as we are able to bear it. For that is what the words and verses in the Bible really are— sure and trustworthy signposts, directing us to the truth.

In themselves they are only words (though inspired words), which we shall only understand gradually as we mature in grace and knowledge through obedience and response to our Lord, who so skillfully chooses the lessons of life for us. When once this great principle is grasped how presumptuous and absurd all dogmatic expounding of the truth and all bitter controversies about it do become.

At first, however, I was far from grasping this fact when I had finished the course at the Bible college. I was as blissfully sure that I now knew and understood the true doctrines of Christianity and all the correct tenets of the faith which I myself must believe and propagate, as I was sure that all other students learning the interpretations of some other school of thought were most certainly misled and in error in all wherein they differed from my own sound doctrine.

I never suspected for a moment that all teachers, be they evangelicals or liberals, fundamentalists or modernists, or of whatever school of thought and to whichever section of the Church they belong, are all alike in one respect and suffer a similar and inescapable dilemma: they cannot enable any one of their students to understand the meaning of the words and the teaching in the Bible. They can point us in the direction they would have us go, they can offer interpretations, right or wrong; they can conscientiously and most clearly expound to us the truths of the Bible as they understand them, and by which they have been helped.

The real meaning of the words and terms which they teach us however, they cannot make us understand, at least not until we have passed through some personal experience by which illumination can come to us.

Everybody knows perfectly well that

though the poets and the writers of every generation have gone to extreme efforts to help us understand what it means to be in love, not until we suddenly fall in love ourselves have we the very slightest conception of the true meaning of the words. When we come to the Bible, the same principle holds true. We can learn the theological definition of the term repentance, but the only people who really know what repentance is are those who have actually experienced it and have truly repented.

In the same way, we only begin to understand what forgiveness is when we realize we have wronged someone and they have forgiven us. But we see a great deal more meaning in the word forgiveness when we ourselves pass through the experience of being deeply wronged and have been taught by the Great Forgiver how to forgive and bear the wrong done to us instead of making the wrongdoer bear it himself.

The one who has been convicted of sin knows far more of the true meaning of the term than does the most learned theologian who has never admitted himself to be in the wrong on any matter at all.

And one who has been saved sees meanings in the words savior and saved, which no one else can fathom. The real meaning of broken-hearted is known only to those whose hearts have actually been broken. It is perfectly impossible for a proud and self-assertive person to have any but the faintest idea of the meaning of meekness until they have themselves been humbled and learned to accept the humiliation.

All these experiences, as they happen to different individuals, take many diverse forms and produce endless variations and degrees of understanding. For example, our Lord himself said that forgiveness will mean one thing to a person conscious of only small offenses, and quite an overwhelmingly different thing to one conscious of having sinned greatly, and still yet a different thing to one who loves and forgives and bears the cost himself.

Yes, the more we think about it, we cannot help realizing that the meaning of words does differ very greatly in different minds, according to our differing stages of experience, and we must face the fact that our words can, and often do, convey totally different ideas to the people we speak to, just as we often distort their words to quite a different sense in our own minds. We might avoid an immense amount of argument and angry feelings and waste of energy if we reminded ourselves of this fact, and checked in ourselves the lust for proving that we are right and the other person wrong.

So as the years pass, and as we are able to bear it, the Lord Jesus, our patient and yet persistent teacher, leads us on into more truth, and will not suffer us to bypass any experience by means of which we can be brought to learn the true meanings of the things which are written in the Scriptures. We are led on day by day, and as we follow the Lord we find with amazed and awed hearts that he is leading us further and ever further into a hitherto undiscovered territory of truth. Regions which for long we never even dimly suspected begin to open up before us in breathtaking beauty and glory, and flooded with a light so dazzling and bright that we can scarcely bear to look, and yet find our whole being aching with a longing to see more and yet more.

The apostle Paul emphasizes this great paradox. Great as was his own understanding of the truth, deepened, strengthened and expanded as it was by his many, many lessons in the school of affliction and sorrow, yet he still knew quite well, even at the end of his life, that "Now we see through a glass darkly; but then it will be face to face: now I know in part, but then I shall know even as I am known" (1 Cor. 13:12).

In our Lord's day there were two schools of thought as far apart in doctrine and teaching as are the fundamentalists and the modernists of today. The orthodox scribes and Pharisees had gathered together, over the course of the years, a great mass of teaching with a fixed and rigid outline of belief and doctrine which, they considered, contained within it the whole truth, and to which nothing could be added. Any new ideas and teaching which did not conform with this standard, or fit in with their rigid dogmas and interpretations, they rejected as heresy.

So that when the Lord Jesus came, with his absolutely revolutionary teaching, emphasizing so forcefully the spirit and not the letter of the law, they realized at once that if these new spiritual conceptions were accepted their whole religious system would be shattered to pieces, simply because it could not possibly contain the new, living, vital truths within its ancient, lifeless and dried-up forms.

Jesus Christ himself gave a vivid and realistic picture of their predicament as they were faced by his challenging and revolutionary teaching. He said that Judaism, as they were practicing it, was like old, shriveled and cracked skin bottles with no elasticity anywhere in them. If anyone tried to pour bubbling, fermenting new wine into such bottles they would certainly burst.

He urged them, therefore, to accept the fact that new ways of expressing the new vital, life-giving message which he had brought were imperative. The old, formal, and dead dogmas, the lifeless ceremonial laws and forms of Judaism, must no longer be forced upon the people, but a new spiritual and mental capacity must be awakened in them in order that they might be able to receive the living truth.

In this twentieth century, Christian orthodoxy does seem to be very much in the same position as was Jewish orthodoxy in our

Lord's day. The more sincere in belief and devoted in wish to glorify our Savior, the more afraid some Christians seem to be of allowing their Lord to lead them into new conceptions of his love and glory and grace. Many seem as deeply suspicious of opening themselves to more light, and as dogmatically determined to accept nothing which they have not hitherto understood and believed, as were the scribes and Pharisees when confronted by the teaching of the Lord of Life himself.

But, as in the parable of the old skin bottles, so now, also, there is the opposite side of the picture. The Sadducees were the moderns and the materialists of their day, and it is really striking to see their counterparts in our times. For if the orthodox are often sincerely afraid to accept any fuller light on the Christian doctrines and to receive new wine into their conceptions of the truth, the moderns seem to have an equal horror and dread of old bottles! They have a passion for trying to sweep away all the lovingly preserved conceptions and traditions of past generations, lumping them altogether all too often, and denouncing them as outworn and incapable of being adapted to the new thought and progressive ideas of today.

In their reaction against the lifeless old bottles, they vigorously endeavor to shatter and explode all the old-fashioned beliefs, and thereby they lose a great deal of priceless and mellowed old wine which might still have been an invaluable enrichment to them.

"New wine," said the Lord, "certainly needs new bottles, but that does not mean that all old bottles must be burst and all the old wine spilled out. Of course not!" It means that the bottles which have become empty and no longer contain any wine at all, but are shriveled and dried up and have allowed all the life to leak out of them—those are the bottles which are useless. "Every scribe that is instructed into the kingdom of heaven is like a man that is an householder, which bringeth out of his treasure things new and old." The wise man is he who thankfully accepts the new wine and just as thankfully retains all that is precious and enriching in the old.

Undoubtedly, as we grow older both in years and in grace and knowledge of the Lord Jesus, we shall find some of the bottles or conceptions which expressed and contained our beliefs in earlier years have become hopelessly inadequate.

Some interpretations we accepted appear shrunken and horribly small for the truth as we now see it, and belief in them is leaking away, if indeed not quite dried up. In that case let us not fear to allow the shriveled bottles to be broken, and to receive from our Lord himself the new spiritual conceptions he is longing to reveal to us, and, if necessary, new ways of expressing them so that others may also be helped by them. Phillip's paraphrase of the Epistles, *Letters to Young Churches*, is a splendid example of this and must have helped many of us.

It is by no means always an easy thing to do, however. Many Christians, who through new and strange experiences of sorrow and testing, have come to see gloriously fuller meaning in some of the Scriptures, are really afraid to share this new light openly with others. For they find with pained and astonished dismay that the immediate reaction of some of the very orthodox among their friends and acquaintances who have either not passed through the same experience (or else have reacted quite differently towards it), is that of suspicion and even antagonism. They may actually find themselves accused of erring from the truth and with some dreadful label attached to them ever after, accusing them of being modernist or crank, heretic or deceived by a lying spirit, or some other term, according to whichever church or school of thought their friends belong to. From then on everything they say will be suspect.

However, at some time or other in the course of our lives each one of us is obliged to pass through some shattering experience which can be likened to Operation Broken Bottles, when everything seems to be breaking up in and around us, and all our old beliefs are shaken and tested to the very foundation. At such times we ought to tell ourselves with thankful confidence that our Lord is allowing everything that can be shaken, to be shaken, so that only that which is real truth remains, and that the distortions which we needed to be freed from are, through this experience, going to be gloriously transformed, just as out of the seed which drops down into death and disintegration there arises a resurrection life.

It is lovely and encouraging too, to many of us, to know that Operation Broken Bottles often occurs in middle life and, later still, at a time when so many who are not Christians are beginning to think drearily that life has already brought them the best it can offer and from now on there can be no more real progress and creativity for them, but only staleness and increasing uselessness.

For the real Christian, Operation Broken Bottles is the forerunner and herald of a tremendous quickening of all their spiritual and creative energies, so that for many, middle and later life prove to be not the end, but the real beginning of fruitfulness and of the most satisfyingly creative period of life, when at last they can say, "My soul is as a weaned child."

"Whom have I in heaven but thee, and there is none upon earth that I desire but thee." Then it comes to pass that our youth is renewed like the eagles, and we who have been crawling and creeping along the way of love amid the frustrations and tests of life, now really begin to "mount up with wings, and to run and not be weary, to walk and not faint." Oh yes, it is glorious beyond words, for then he begins to pour new wine into new bottles, and a new phase in our Christian and spiritual life begins, a maturing into the heavenly and eternal life.

How tragic it is that so many Christians do not realize this. They are still afraid of any new light, and instead of opening themselves more and more fully during these middle years, in joyful expectancy, they become more and more rigid and contracted in their spiritual understanding, and miss the whole lovely experience which is the right of every Christian in the forties and the fifties and increasingly as long as life shall last. If conversion is like blossom time, then this experience of receiving new wine into new bottles, whether earlier or later in life, is like the time of the ripe fruit.

Sometimes, however, when I try to share with others some of these new glorious ideas and facets of the truth (but the more one reads the books by earlier Christians, the more one realizes that no part of the truth is new, and conceptions which seem new to us were, and are, known to others, but have just been mislaid in our own particular Christian circle!) These friends sometimes say, "Wherever did you pick up that idea? I can't think where you find it in the Bible. Show me chapter and verse to prove it."

But that is just what one cannot do! One

cannot turn to a particular chapter and verse and say triumphantly: "There it is! Don't you see in it what I have now come to see? And, indeed, countless other verses in the Scriptures now seem bursting with this same meaning and truth where I never noticed or suspected it before. Surely you must see it too!"

But it is very likely that they won't. For the meaning of words is only learned in the school of affliction, and we don't all learn the same parts of the truth in the same order. We cannot, therefore, expect anyone to see what we see, unless they have been where we have been, any more than we can see what has been revealed to others who have been learning another part of the truth in some quite different sort of experience.

All we do know is, that after certain experiences of obedience and acceptance of the will of God, perhaps of becoming acquainted with grief in some new and more poignant way, or after losing our heart's desire, or through physical suffering and illness—suddenly, perhaps, or gradually and almost imperceptibly, new and fuller and richer meanings reveal themselves in many great passages of Scripture where before we had only seen the particular meaning which we had been taught to read into it.

We do not un-see what we saw before, only now it opens out into such a vast realm of glory and wonder and light, that our former understanding of that particular thing now seems so dwarfed that it is like looking at some lovely view through a pinpoint in a card. To think as we thought before seems so inadequate (though it was a part of the truth) that the former idea is almost swallowed up and lost.

So I cannot, and I do not say to you in this book, "You must really try to see what I have seen." But what I do say to everyone, and I say it with a heart full of joy and love and thankfulness, is this:

Oh, don't you want to see much more than you have seen?

Then let us encourage one another to go exploring further along the way of glad obedience to God and acceptance of his will, whereby the eyes of our understanding will be enlightened; keeping open to all the new light which he longs to give us, and no longer fearfully telling ourselves that he may allow us to be deceived and led into error if we consider new conceptions and ideas not already familiar to us.

For has not our Lord himself said to all sincerely hungry and thirsty souls and minds, who long to know him better, but who dread that the enemy may be allowed to take advantage of this longing:

"If a son ask bread of his father, will he give him a stone? or if he ask for fish, will he give him a serpent? How much more shall your heavenly Father give the Holy Spirit to them that ask him." And the Holy Spirit, we know, is given that he may "lead us into all truth."

Yes, all the experiences of life are planned and permitted with one unspeakably glorious purpose in view, that we may follow on to know the Lord, whom to know is life eternal. And those who follow on, find indeed that,

"The path of the just is as a shining light, which shineth more and more unto the perfect day" (Prov. 4:18).

CHAPTER 3
Through Death to Life

"God forbid that I should glory save in the cross of our Lord Jesus Christ by whom the world is crucified unto me and I unto the world" (Gal. 6:4).

"I am crucified with Christ, nevertheless I live; yet not I but Christ liveth in me, and the life which I now live in the flesh, I live by the faith of the Son of God who loved me and gave himself for me" (Gal. 2:20).

In the Gospels and the Epistles we are given some lovely glimpses of life in the heavenly places, where it is the purpose of our Savior that each one of his followers should live. We are shown that he calls us up to a new plane of life altogether, where perfect love is the one law, and where we are so completely transformed through the renewing of our minds that we literally become new creatures in whom the Holy Spirit of love makes his dwelling place, just as he dwelt in our Lord and Savior.

It is made plain that he wishes to use all our yielded faculties to their utmost capacity so that he can think his thoughts in our minds and then be free to express them through our lips and in lovely actions towards others. We know that we are meant to enjoy the winged life of those who have access to the heavenly places just as truly as the birds have access to the sky.

Now we must consider the way up to the heavenly places, the starting point of the track which we must follow on the wings of obedient faith and response to our Lord Jesus Christ.

There is no escape from the truth (which at first so dismays our hearts) that the cross is the gateway to the heavenly places and that death is the way into true life. We must pass through death ourselves if we want to mount up into the realms of life and light and love. The Cross does stand at the very heart and center of the Christian life—the cross of our Lord and Savior Jesus Christ, by which he achieved our deliverance from the bondage of sin and self-love and opens to us the means of sharing in his own life.

The cross of the Savior has many glorious aspects and mysteries too deep to fathom, but one aspect we must not, indeed, cannot escape, namely that his cross is a double cross, for himself and for his followers. We cannot truly say that the Savior does everything for us unless we at once go on to acknowledge that though everything for our salvation comes to us as a gift of God's grace, it must now be worked out in each one of us individually.

The results of Christ's death cannot accomplish our deliverance from the power of sin unless they now result in the death and crucifixion of our own self life. The treatment and the cure of the terrible disease of sin which is offered to us by the Savior, do depend for their saving effect upon our willingness to allow him to take us through the very same experience of death to self.

We know by actual experience that his death on the cross was not a substitution for our own physical death (for we all die), and neither was it a substitution for this dying to our selves. But by his death on the cross he has revealed to us the means by which he is able to heal the disease of sin in the whole body of mankind and effect a complete cure.

When he, the Son of God, became Son of Man through complete identity with the whole sin-perishing human race, he met sin in all its awful power as it worked its deadly havoc in the whole body, and overcame it. He made himself sin bearer—not sin avenger. Day by day throughout his life on earth he manifested forth this glorious truth, by accepting and bearing every conceivable wrong against himself, and reacting to it with love and forgiveness. He rejected all the daily temptations to break the royal law of love and to begin loving himself more than others.

He faced every temptation possible to human beings, and he showed that the only way to overcome these temptations was to allow the Holy Spirit of love to control his thoughts and his feelings and to show him how to react with perfect love under every circumstance. He denied himself and took up his cross daily, and this was the principle he commanded his followers. His great method for obtaining victory was to overcome evil with good. If he had refused to do this or had ceased to be the Lamb of God who bore the sin of the world, if he had begun avenging himself on those who sinned against him, or if he had tried to evade the whole experience, he would have failed, just as we fail, and he would have had no victory and no overcoming power to offer us.

He practiced and openly demonstrated this triumphant reaction to evil, for thirty-three years, and then on the cross, the veil was torn apart and the full truth was revealed to men, namely that the Son of God who is also Son of Man, is the second Adam, the head of the whole body of mankind, and as such, he is able to overcome triumphantly all the awful power of sin's disease in the human race and to overrule all its ghastly effects and results, and to reconcile all things to God.

For through his resurrection from the dead, this greatest and most glorious truth of the gospel was revealed to us, that he is able to destroy the works of the devil, to conquer death, which is the result of the disease of sin, and to raise up the whole body of mankind and to share in his resurrection life with all who are willing to receive it and will respond to him in faith and love and obedience.

But (and on this point we must be careful to make no mistake), the cure of our sin does depend upon our willingness to go the same way that he went. He can only save us from our sins by enabling us to react under every circumstance of our lives in the very same way in which he reacted under all the circumstances of his life, namely, in love and forgiveness and death to our own selves. A cure has been discovered and made available but the treatment is drastic and must be accepted and followed. The apostle Paul stated it uncompromisingly: "I am crucified with Christ."

It is in the daily circumstances of our lives that we are put to death. We cannot choose the way in which we are to be crucified, we can only accept the means of dying to self which each day brings us, at the hands of those with whom we live and work, and through all that is utterly uncongenial and repugnant to our own self-love; the things we don't like and want to evade, the frustrations and disappointments and heartbreaks, as well as the wrongdoings of others the results of which fall upon us. This dying is a process.

"Many dyings and many deaths," until, as William Law says, "The spirit of love really becomes alive in us" and possesses us fully. But—and this is the glorious part—all the time that we are dying to self we may know heaven at the same time. At first, certainly, the dying is terribly painful and we struggle and resist, but sooner or later (depending upon how fully and quickly we yield ourselves and our will in all the daily circumstances of life) there comes a crisis when the real resurrection begins.

It is a strange paradox—resurrection, but still a daily dying! For the dying really is this process of having our thought life transformed. We die to all unloving thoughts and allow the Holy Spirit of love to substitute his thoughts. Therefore, the continual dying is, as it were, the real root of our life in the heavenly places. It is through the door of death that we pass out from the prison of self and can swoop up into the glorious joy and liberty of the heavenly places.

The psalmist has beautifully expressed this experience in these words: "Our soul is escaped as a bird out of the snare of the fowlers: the snare is broken and we are escaped" (Psa. 124:7).

In one sense we are never off the cross, and yet at the same time we are always exulting in the winged life of heaven, for by the daily, delighted laying down of self-love we are enabled to rise up in the power of Christ and to love all as ourselves. This, surely, is what heaven really is, the congregation of all those who are made perfect in love. The cross is indeed the ladder set up on earth and reaching up to heaven; it is the door into the heavenly places.

It may be that there are some reading this chapter who exclaim to themselves, sorrowfully and almost despairingly: "But I have been praying for years for this death to my self, this crucifixion of my old nature, but it never takes place."

There are two possible reasons for such a situation. The first is that we are not always willing to accept the particular cross which the Lord has chosen for us! I think it was Oswald Chambers who said: "It wouldn't be so difficult for us to agree to crucifixion if we could choose our own cross and arrange for the right onlookers to be watching!" But crucifixion is a terribly lonely thing, and sometimes we spend years trying to evade the particular cross which the Lord has chosen to be the doorway into the heavenly places for us.

For many it will be the suffering of na-

35

ture's longings which can never know satisfaction, the acceptance of the fact that marriage is not for them and that they must, perhaps, learn to love without being loved in return; willingness to accept year after year a drab uninteresting existence, or to care for someone it is difficult to love, and who yet absorbs all our time and strength and makes it impossible for us to fulfill ourselves as we long to do.

Uncongenial fellow workers, especially those who are dominating and narrow and above all, obstructive, can prove very adequate nails to hold us to the cross which the Lord has chosen for us. Learning to react creatively to all these things (which is the subject of the next chapter), is the only way by which this dying to self becomes real and actual in our lives.

But there is a second point to remember: This process of being put to death is often a long drawn out process and the particular cross may be allowed to continue for years. But in that case resurrection can be simultaneous, as soon as we really submit to, and accept with all our will, the circumstances which are so difficult or frustrating or agonizing.

It seems, however, that in the majority of cases, there does come a special crisis, some particular experience of special suffering or testing, involving an uttermost surrender. And when that point is reached, then the rising together with Christ really does begin.

Either the circumstances which have been God's means of bringing us to the point of real death to self are changed and we come down from the cross, or else those circumstances cease to be an anguish to us and are changed into the very wings by means of which we mount up joyously and triumphantly into the heavenly places.

The main point to remember, however, is that until there is willing acceptance of the circumstances which we have tried so desperately to evade or to alter, there can be no winged life, because the dying is not yet complete. For many and many a child of God the victory has come and the winged life has commenced when at last they have been willing to say: "I will accept So-and-So just as they are, and will stop trying to alter them and to escape from the demands which they make upon me. From now on I choose to bear and to love."

But in the next chapter we shall be considering this matter more fully, for it is when we learn to react creatively to all the sufferings of life that the winged life really begins.

CHAPTER 4

Power to Become Creative

"Bread corn is bruised ... but no one crushes it forever" (Isa. 28:28, Authorized version and Dr. Moffatt).

The prophet Isaiah reminds us that corn must be bruised and broken to pieces, and be ground into fine flour, before it can be used to satisfy the needs of others, but he goes on to add: "but no one bruises it and grinds it forever—only until it is so utterly broken and ground to pieces, that it is fit for the highest use for which it was designed."

This being the case with ordinary corn, we may be quite sure that the Creator, our Lord Jesus Christ, does not allow any breaking and shattering process in our lives without design. But when the bruising times come along (and they come again and again to all of us in the course of life) it is really a signal for awed joy and thanksgiving, for he who loves us is evidently preparing us for further and lovelier uses; and expects us peacefully to believe his words to Peter: "What I do thou knowest not now, but thou shalt know hereafter" (John 13:7).

So much, however, depends upon how we react to these experiences which Love himself has designed for our enrichment, and whether we allow him to teach us the secret of creative reaction instead of just resigned submission, or the tragically destructive reaction of self-pity, resentment and bitterness. There seem to be definite principles which the bruised corn must learn and practice, if it is to be made bread corn for the use of others.

The first is this: The secret of victorious Christian living and creative power is to go through each day praising God for everything; the bad things as well as the good.

As I look back over the past few years of my own life I am astonished beyond words by two things. First, the complete transformation in my whole life, outlook, inner experience and most of all in my own character, as well as my bodily health, which has resulted from the practice of this one simple principle, i.e., to react to everything with praise and thanksgiving instead of with grumbling and moaning and protest and resistance.

Second, the extraordinary fact that I had lived as a Christian and a missionary, among so many other Christians and missionaries, and for so many years, without realizing that this is a vital Christian principle and the very first principle for becoming fruitful and creative. For of course it is written again and again throughout the whole New Testament, and how could so many of us have been so blind! The apostle Paul and the other writers reiterate it almost to the point of laying themselves open to the charge of unnecessary repetition, but evidently in their experience of human nature and of Christian practice, they knew it needed to be constantly emphasized:

"Rejoice evermore," "and again I say rejoice!" "My brethren, count it all joy when ye fall into divers temptations." "We rejoice in infirmities and tribulations." And a host of other passages. Even the Old Testament saints knew this principle. "Whoso offereth praise glorifieth me, and prepareth a way by which I may show him my salvation" (Psa. 50:23).

Yet I had never really grasped this. Of course I knew it was only right and proper to be grateful to God for the nice things that happened, and for all answers to prayer and for his gracious overrulings. But it never once entered my head that a Christian is one who reacts to everything with praise and thanksgiving and joy, and thereby receives power to bring good out of evil. Yes, even to react to the activities and thwartings of the great enemy himself with praise and rejoicing and thereby be made so creative that out of his plans and machinations we can fashion lovely reactions and victories for the glory of God.

Even when, by the help and grace of the Savior, I began quite deliberately and conscientiously to practice this principle of praising for everything, I did not understand how it worked nor why we were to do it. Indeed, it looked quite absurd and almost hypocritical when one was feeling so different, perhaps so completely overwhelmed by something which had happened which seemed to be everything that was wrong and contradictory to God's will and promises.

But I soon began to see how it worked, and then to grasp the full significance of the difference between creative reaction and destructive reaction to all the happenings of life. And though at first there were some dreadful occasions when the testings seemed so terribly overwhelming that I did not praise, I began to realize very quickly that the practice of this principle produced a power in me and such startling and magnificent results as I had never before supposed possible.

The more it is practiced, the more power it creates, until I found my whole body reacting differently too, as though every part of my physical nature had been quickened and rejuvenated as much as my mind. It was a revolutionary and glorious experience, and oh, what a shame that so many of us who are Christians either never hear about it or decide not to practice it!

But there is a second principle the bruised corn must also practice; namely this: don't try to hold on to anything in this life, but willingly let go, in order to be able to receive new enrichment from the Lord.

Once, after a time of very special nervous strain and sorrow, the Lord graciously strengthened and restored me by a beautiful holiday alone with himself among the mountains. On the last day of that holiday I stood near the summit of one of the mountains and looked out on the glorious view spread before me, and for a moment an aching longing filled me: "Oh, if only I could stay here always in the peace and quiet and beauty and healing joy of thy presence, with no interruptions and no distractions. If only this, too, did not have to be taken from me as everything else has been taken away."

But instantly there came the quiet, loving reply from the Lord himself:

Don't try to hold on to this mountaintop experience. Indeed, never try to hold on to anything, but let go immediately and willingly in order to be ready to receive the new joys and riches which I am preparing for you."

Then I understood vividly, for the first time, how vital and how precious this principle is. In the experience of sorrow and loss there is indeed great pain, but if there is no bitterness and no resentment or self-pity mixed with it, it is a clean and healing pain with no poison in it. The real bitterness and unbearable pain in sorrow and loss, lie in trying to hold on to the things we can no longer keep, in the refusal to let go willingly, in the desperate and frantic clinging to the objects which we treasure, the idols of our hearts.

We suffer so intolerably in mind (and often, as result, in body also), because of this passionate clinging to the familiar objects of our love which have so twined themselves into our hearts that the thought of being severed from them is a torment and a horror to us. Pain and anguish there must be, in bereavement—but not torment. Torment is the result of refusing to give them up, and sometimes we suffer almost intolerably and quite unnecessarily when we are forced to relinquish even worthless objects and will not acquiesce in the loss.

But "in acceptance lieth peace" as Amy Carmichael told us, and in the willingness to let go (as he gives us strength to do it), and by opening ourselves to receive what he has chosen for us instead lies a joy which nothing else can give and a peace which nothing in the world can either give or take away. While we practice these two principles we become, quite literally, invulnerable. There is nothing that can harm us, though of course there are many things which will still be able to cause pain, but it will be pain which itself is healing and blessed.

There is yet a third principle for becoming creative in eternal things, and that is, everything that is willingly laid down into death will be raised to life again in some more glorious and perfect form.

"Except a corn of wheat fall into the ground and die, it abideth alone, but if it die it bringeth forth much fruit."

Everything that is willingly laid down for love's sake bears in it the germ of resurrection life. It is the things that we feel we cannot and will not lay down into death, which are finally and inexorably forced from us, and which bear in themselves the seed of a death which can experience no resurrection. For the worms of bitterness and resentment and self-pity have eaten into the heart of them and destroyed the seed of life. That which is forced away from us is lost to us indeed, but that which is willingly laid down into death will be raised to life again in the form of some lovely creative activity and power which we have never before possessed.

Many who read this chapter will know far more than I do about this matter, for you have learned more advanced lessons in the school of life. Perhaps also there will be some to whom this chapter will prove a seed of life, because you read it just at the right time, when such a message as this will be love's own word to meet your condition. You are longing to find the way by which your frustrated life and instincts and powers may become creative and not be wasted and apparently unneeded.

Lay every frustrated and unsatisfied instinct and ability which you possess, down into death, and your Lord and Savior will raise them up again in forms of creative energy and power which you did not before possess or know how to use. For it seems that "dying," in and through the circumstances he permits to happen to us, is the only way to real creative activity and fullest satisfaction and the power to bring into being something that will be to the praise of God forever.

In actual experience we do find (though often not for months or even years afterwards) that the things which we willingly laid down into death, when they are raised up again become the means and channels through which God quickens life and power in other people, in marvelous ways of which we had never dreamed. It seems, in fact, that dying, in some form or other, is the only way by which God can produce in us really creative activity—the power to create and bring into being something which will outlast our mortal lives and share in eternity.

Learning to practice this great principle is one of the chief purposes of our life here on earth. We who are made in the image of God the Creator are brought into this world to share the experiences of human life, so that we may be taught by him how to become creative too. It is, therefore, intensely important that we should understand that the material out of which we are to create is the sorrow and suffering and disappointment and frustration of this life, and all its difficult testings and circumstances. Yes, sorrow is the material which we are to use. At first, perhaps, it was not so.

In Eden, Adam and Eve might have learned to become creators using another material altogether, namely experiences of good unmixed with evil. But then they could never have created the glorious and unique realities which it is our privilege to produce ever since mortal life on earth became an experience of knowing good and evil. They could never have known true joy, for joy is sorrow accepted and overcome, and peace comes into being through the acceptance of fear and anxiety and restlessness and uncertainty and insecurity.

Love is a far more burning and holy and Godlike thing than Adam and Eve could ever have known in Eden, for Christlike love is created in us when we accept the hatred and the malice and the wrongdoing of others, and bear it, and through forgiveness, overcome and transform it. So, with all the other evils resulting from the sin of unlovingness, we produce lovelier jewels for the foundation of the New Jerusalem in the crucible of pain and sorrow than could possibly have been produced in any other way.

When Adam and Eve chose to eat of the Tree of the Knowledge of Good and Evil, the material out of which all their sons and daughters were to create was changed completely. Since then it has been true, not only of physical procreation, but of every kind of real creative experience, that "I will greatly multiply thy sorrow and conception; in sorrow thou shalt bring forth" (Gen. 3:11).

"But where sin abounded, grace doth much more abound," and it does not matter that our chief creative material is now sorrow and pain, for we find, just as the Lord Jesus himself so gloriously demonstrated, that we can fashion out of it things infinitely more glorious and more to the delight and praise of God, than would otherwise have been possible; though of course at infinitely more cost both to himself and to ourselves.

His design for us is that we shall become co-workers and co-creators with himself in the unutterably wonderful work of bringing good out of evil, and fashioning loveliness and power and life out of things which have been distorted, deformed and smitten by death.

It is absolutely plain that there are, in fact, but two ways of dealing with evil. There is the best way possible to ordinary human beings: the way of trying to bind it, imprison it, and render it harmless and incapable of expressing itself in ways destructive to the happiness and peace of others. So we punish evildoers and, when necessary and possible, we confine them and restrain their activities by force. But this is a very inadequate and unsuccessful way, for it leaves the evildoers completely unchanged or even worse than before.

The other way, God's way, revealed to us by Jesus Christ, is the triumphant and perfectly successful way of overcoming evil by good. This means accepting it, bearing it, and reacting to it in such a way, and with such love and forgiveness, that either we succeed in transforming the evil thing itself into a good and beautiful thing, or else we can produce out of it some glorious and lovely thing which we did not before possess; for example patience, courage, endurance, joy and the most beautiful jewels of all, forgiveness and compassionate love.

Perhaps the only things which can really live forever and be taken over into eternity with us, are the evil things which our Savior and Lord has enabled us to transform into good and beautiful things. I love to think that the jewels which we are told form the very foundation of the heavenly Jerusalem are all the experiences of this life to which we have reacted in such a way that they are transformed into lasting glories and radiant beauties; jewels wrought out of sorrow and anguish and brought forth in the furnace of affliction. How privileged we are! How unspeakably fortunate, when we learn this glorious truth and yield ourselves to the skill and power of our Savior. For "He that overcometh shall inherit all things" (Rev. 21:7).

These, then, are the principles which, when we practice them by his grace and power, make us new creatures and produce in us the power to become creative—in our thoughts and work and Christian witness, in a way which we would never have believed to be possible: 1) Go through each day praising for everything, 2) Don't try to hold on to anything in this life, but willingly let go, in order to be able to receive new enrichment from the Lord, 3) Everything that is willingly laid down into death will be raised to life in some radiant new form and with creative power.

These are the means by which the creative instinct in us, often so thwarted, frustrated, unsatisfied and distorted, can find its true outlet and rise from death to resurrection life, transforming every part of our nature, physical, mental and spiritual, and enabling us to create beauties and glories and love which will live forever. So that, over and over again our lonely, frustrated or broken hearts will find themselves singing with amazed and adoring thankfulness,

"Sing, O barren, thou that didst not bear; break forth into singing and cry aloud, thou that didst not travail with child. For more are the children of the desolate than the children of the married wife, saith the Lord" (Isa. 54:1).

CHAPTER 5
Transformed Thought Life

"Be ye transformed by the renewing of your mind" *(Rom. 12:2).*

"Casting down imaginations and every high thing that exalteth itself against the knowledge of God, and bringing into captivity every thought—to the obedience of Christ" (2 Cor. 10:5).

If we are to know anything about the winged life in the heavenly places we must indeed begin a new phase of life, and as Paul puts it, be transformed and rise to a completely different plane of Christian living. It is very much the same kind of experience that happens to young fledglings when the time comes for them to leave the nest and learn to fly and mount up into the sky as their parents do.

Probably the real winged life is not normal or even possible for us at the beginning of our Christian life. There must be a certain degree of growth and development first (through learning to die to self), and while we are still absolutely dependent upon others for our spiritual food we shall not be able to use our wings and mount up into the new and radiant realm of the high places of the kingdom of heaven.

But our Lord and Savior undertakes to teach us the winged life just as soon as we are ready for it, and this he does by going to the very root and heart of our trouble, the thought life. As long as that remains wrong we are still completely earthbound. But when we allow him to begin transforming us by the renewing of our minds, then we begin the winged life.

The Greek word for repentance is a word which literally means change your thoughts. Stop thinking as you have been, and begin thinking about everything quite differently. Our greatest need is to begin a completely new kind of thought life, for there is the very heart and center of our problem. It is there that the seeds of sin begin.

"As a man thinketh in his heart, so is he."
It is in our thoughts that all sin (which is love centered upon ourselves) has its roots, and it is there that we need to experience the salvation and deliverance which the Savior offers.

We have never said or done an ungracious or un-Christlike word or action which was not first an ungracious and un-Christlike thought. We have never felt dislike or hate for a person without first of all thinking thoughts of dislike which have grown into hate. We have never committed a visible act of sin which has shamed us before others, which was not first a shameful thought. We have never wronged another person without first wronging them many times in our thoughts. For what we habitually think will, sooner or later, manifest itself clearly in some visible expression of that thought.

The same thing is equally true about loving, compassionate, kind and Christ-inspired thoughts. They all express themselves, without any effort on our part. They come forth and reveal themselves as naturally and easily and simply as the unfolding of a flower. All outward living is the natural expression of our inward thinking; of the much more real world of our thought life.

No wonder that we need to learn the lovely transforming secret of a thought life brought completely and unbrokenly under the control of the Holy Spirit of Love. For love truly begins in our thoughts and not in our feelings. Our feelings follow our thoughts and, according to our thought habits, so will our feelings be.

Here is a simple illustration which everyone can verify quite easily from their own experience, especially in youth! You meet someone who captures your imagination (not at first your feelings), a handsome, attractive and charming man, or a beautiful, fascinating and gracious girl.

When once your imagination has been captured you think of that person continually; your thoughts revolve around them and keep reverting back to them, but always they are delightful thoughts about the beauty and charm, or the courage and the strength of that particular person. And as you think happy, admiring and delighted thoughts about them, so the corresponding feelings awaken in you, feelings of pleasure and delight and a thrill of joy for every remembrance; and before you know where you are you have fallen in love. Your feelings have followed the pattern of your thoughts, and as they were admiring and delightful thoughts, so the feelings are delightful too.

But once begin to change your thoughts about that person, as perhaps quickly happens on closer acquaintance; once begin thinking to yourself, "I don't believe he is as nice as I first supposed; he really seems utterly selfish," or "She has a beautiful face, but I think she is very vain and a great flirt and only lives for admiration," and you will find yourself falling out of love as quickly as you fell in. Your feelings will be changed completely by the change in your thoughts.

All too often this happens after marriage, and then the new, disparaging thought habits become fixed by daily contact and the changed feelings become just as firmly fixed. If only disillusioned lovers would realize this and repent and change their thoughts yet a third time (not back to the first illusions), but to quite a different kind of thought, namely a longing to love and to be a helpmeet, and to rejoice in the creative power of love to change what is unlovely in others, and to delight in loving even if we are not loved in return; then all the hurt, humiliated, furious and resentful feelings of dislike or hate would change into compassion and loving desire to help the other partner.

Yes, our feelings do follow our thoughts, and as we think, so we are. Nothing is truer than this fact and, at the same time, nothing more absurd than the widespread belief that we can hide our thought habits from other people. It really is extraordinary how we tell ourselves that as long as we do not express our thoughts in words, nobody can possibly know anything about them and they remain safely hidden.

No greater fallacy can be imagined. Every single person in the world, except those who know what it is to have every thought brought into captivity to Christ, would be appalled if thought-reading became possible and universal, or if someone invented an apparatus by which all our innermost, secret thoughts could be projected onto a screen for everybody to see. Nevertheless, nothing is plainer than the fact that all our thoughts will out, and our friends and acquaintances and those with whom we live, know and appraise us entirely according to our thought habits.

We all know one another's thought habits perfectly well, and sum them up when we speak about each other. "So-and-so," we say, "is a very attractive girl, but frightfully vain and conceited." Now, so and so has never told us by word of mouth that she thinks she is fascinatingly pretty and that everybody falls for her charms, but, our summing up of her character simply means that we are well aware that she must spend an enormous amount of time thinking about her appearance and what she is going to wear and how she can enhance her attractiveness.

Again, we say, "So-and-so is a miserly old creature and it is no use asking him for anything to help advance the Lord's work." Now old so-and-so has probably never told anyone in words that he is a miser and loves hoarding his money and loathes giving it away, but quite obviously all his thoughts do center on his money, planning how to scrimp and save, and denying himself this and that pleasure—and charity!—in order to add to his bank balance.

And when our friends say: "Isn't it a pity that so-and-so, with all her activities in Christian work and witness, is so ungracious, so bad-tempered and critical of others," what we really mean is: "Isn't it a pity that so-and-so continually thinks ungracious and critical and ugly things about her friends and the people around her." It is obvious, when we stop to think about it, that we do know each other by our inner thought habits, for these simply will out. When we say, "Ah! she is a perfect dear, always so kind, and willing to help," we may be sure that the thought life of that one is full of kind and loving thoughts and of desire to help those around her.

Thought must, and does, express itself in a multitude of ways, entirely apart from our own choice and desire. People who are slaves to impure thoughts, even though they may hate those thoughts (as well as being helplessly fascinated by them), cannot hide this bondage either, for in many involuntary ways it is quite easily recognized by those with eyes to see.

As we think, so we are, and so we are known and judged by those around us.

It is strange that so many Christians think salvation means only being saved from a future judgment and condemnation. They fail to realize that it also means being saved and delivered here and now from all these wrong thought habits, and being so changed as a result, that there will be no future judgment and condemnation necessary.

When the Holy Spirit of love dwells in us he teaches us how to use all our faculties and all the members of our body in harmony with the law of holy love. This is the salvation which Christ offers. He is called Jesus (Savior) because he saves us from a sin-diseased thought life and gives us his own power to think the creative thoughts of love and to express them continually, without effort, or struggle and strain, but easily and simply and with great power. When the thought life is really transformed the whole outward life is transformed also as a natural consequence.

We need to remind ourselves that love is wonderfully creative and so are all the thoughts of love. Those who experience the transformed thought life discover more and more clearly that they are in touch with forces which have a worldwide influence, and are contacting completely new powers and energies.

Change your thoughts about that diffi-cult, exasperating, cranky or hardhearted person with whom you must live or work, and you are well on the way to helping them to a complete change too, without any need for you to buttonhole or tackle them. Love them in your thoughts and express that love, and in nine cases out of ten, when they are in your presence they will begin to be new people. You will have the effect upon them that people have on you when you know they love you.

But just as you never feel at your best and act your best in the presence of those who disapprove of you, so others will be at their very worst in your presence if they know that you are continually criticizing and disapproving of them in your thoughts. "I know the thoughts that I think toward you, saith the Lord of Hosts, thoughts of peace and not of evil to give you an expected end." How creative his thoughts are! What a change they bring about in us.

This does not mean that we are to shut our eyes to the faults and blemishes in others, nor are we to condone them, or to tell ourselves that we are mistaken in thinking that those faults are present. No, love is very clear-sighted and does discern these things, but she reacts to them as a compassionate nurse or doctor reacts to the horrible symptoms in a cancer patient. The symptoms of sin are ugly and loathsome, but the reaction which they call forth in the love-controlled disciple of Jesus Christ is a longing desire to share and to bear and to heal.

We should never concentrate in thought or prayer on the faults and failings and sins and stumblings of others, but on the power of love of the Savior to heal and change. We should see these needy people as they will be when they have been healed and transformed and we should pray for that lovely vision to come true as quickly as possible.

Our thoughts so quickly awaken feelings in us, and our feelings make themselves so obvious, that if we dwell on the mistakes of others we shall always be irritated by them, and while we feel irritated and unwilling to accept and bear with these people as they are, they will be conscious of it and will be closed to any help from us.

Most likely, however, they will automatically open to the help and the love which they so need, when we ourselves are so full of creative love that all exasperated thoughts and feelings are excluded.

Of course there will be some exceptions, just as there were some people who would not respond to the Lord himself. But he did not allow that to change his love or to influence his feeling towards them, and in the end, we may be sure, love will prevail.

Once again there may be some who, at this point, are saying to themselves nearly despairingly: "It all sounds too good to be true, and exactly what I need and long for. But such a transformation in my thought life seems impossible, for all my habits are so firmly fixed that I am in complete bondage to them, and it is as much as I can do to refrain from thinking the wrong kind of thoughts for more than an hour or two at a time. I just cannot see how such a glorious transformation can take place in me."

But it certainly can. There are, however, some very important things to remember in connection with a transformed thought life, and these we are to consider in the next chapter.

CHAPTER 6

Keys to Victory in The Thought Life

"Finally, brethren, whatsoever things are true, whatsoever things are honest, whatsoever things are just, whatsoever things are pure, whatsoever things are lovely, and whatsoever things are of good report; if there be any virtue and if there be any praise, think on these things" (Phil. 4:8).

In our day and generation ever so many Christians seem terribly conscious that they are not experiencing the kind of grace and power and victory which the promises in the

New Testament had led them to expect would be theirs when they began to follow the Lord Jesus Christ. They wonder why, and how it is that the good news of the gospel does not seem to work out in their own experience the lovely and wonderful transformation of character which it claims to produce in those who respond to the Savior.

When this subject of a transformed thought life is mentioned, over and over again even the most earnest and sincere Christian workers exclaim: "But how does it become real in actual fact? How did you yourself find the power to overcome your old thought habits and to begin practicing completely different ones? Do tell me the secret of how I, too, may be transformed by the renewing of my mind."

In one of the chapters in *The Kingdom of Love* I tried to answer these questions, not very successfully I think, and without making it as clear as I could have wished. I think perhaps this was because I shrank from sharing in too personal a way things which some might feel ought to remain a secret between the Lord and the individual soul.

Many people, and with very good reason, have a great distrust of sharing their inner experiences, and certainly there are many which we ought not to share and even which we risk losing if we do parade them before others. But there are some things which other Christians are desperately longing to know and which they need to be told, and if we know at least a part of the answer to their problems and questions, it must be right to share with them what we do know.

The Lord's very last injunction to his followers was, "Ye shall be witnesses unto me." Now a witness may only legitimately give evidence about things which he has actually witnessed and experienced himself, and not a word of what he only knows by hearsay, unless he clearly states that it was told him by others. So in this chapter I want to try and share more fully and clearly the secret keys which I discovered in my own experience did unlock, as it were, the door of the power house and enabled me to make actual contact moment by moment with the victorious, overcoming power of the Savior himself, just as we are promised in the New Testament.

In Judges we have a story which seems to throw very significant and challenging light on this whole matter of witnessing and sharing with others. It is both a warning of the wrong way, and a clear indication of the right way. We read of Samson, the strongest man who ever lived, and many times this question was asked of him:

"Tell me, I pray thee, wherein thy great strength lieth?"

Time and again Samson refused to comply with the request, until at last he succumbed to the importunity and revealed the means by which he could be deprived of that strength, and in that revealing and wrong sharing he brought about his own downfall.

I think that many of us feel that this is a true warning, and greatly fear that if we begin talking about our inner spiritual experience and parade before others the secret of contact with the source of all strength, we shall find that we break the contact or cause a puncture of some kind through which the power will leak away and leave us bereft of the victory which we have so confidently and rejoicingly testified about to others.

Now there certainly is very real danger in talking about our own power and victory in the Christian life, especially in the way we are tempted to do it as a means of self-display.

But in actual fact it was not wrong for Samson to share with others the secret source of his great power, but the tragedy lay in telling it to the wrong person and under the wrong circumstances. Everybody in Israel, and everyone among his own friends and acquaintances, knew as a matter of course the secret of his great strength—indeed it could not possibly be called a secret—for they all realized that it lay in the fact that he had been a Nazarite all his life long, namely a person completely set apart to love and serve God, with no rival claims or ties to interfere with his service.

The sign of this separation was open and visible for all to see: no razor had ever come upon his head and his hair was long and uncut. Everyone in Israel who met him, knew at once, without having to be told, that it was no use to offer him wine or any part of the grape, and that he would never touch a dead body. There were things he could not do as long as his hair remained uncut. And when they heard from others of his great and miraculous power, it must have been instantly clear to them that the two things went together, separation to God and God-given strength.

So that when Samson told Delilah that the secret of his strength lay in his long hair, he was not really telling her the whole truth any more than in his previous answers; for his strength did not lie in his unshaven locks, but in the separation to God which they symbolized. It was when he allowed himself to be beguiled into sleeping in the presence of his enemies and when he allowed Delilah to put herself in the place of God, that he broke his contact with the source of his strength and became weak as other men and helpless in the hands of those who hated him.

In the same way it is not, of course, dangerous to witness to the fact that our true source of strength is in the Lord Jesus Christ, but we put ourselves in the power of the enemy when we do it just to show off and to draw attention to the wonderful way in which God uses us in his service. Too often we do it in the wrong place and to the wrong people and in the wrong way!

The secret of the great strength which we all need, just as much as did Samson, lies in willingness to be a Nazarite unto the Lord, wholly set apart for his use. It means that we agree with the Lord that his Holy Spirit is to be allowed to dwell in us and use every faculty and power that we possess in the way that he chooses, just as our Savior chose the same thing. The apostle Paul expresses it in this way:

"I beseech you . . . that ye present your bodies a living sacrifice unto God . . . and that ye be transformed by the renewing of your mind, that he may prove (experience) what it is to have working in you continually, the good and acceptable and perfect will of God" (Rom. 12:1, 2).

Now if this transforming experience is to become real in us there are definite conditions to be fulfilled, a principle of obedient response and separation as real and necessary as the law of the Nazarite in the Old Testament. There are vows to be made, and we must allow the Holy Spirit to reveal to each one of us individually the things which he knows will hinder him from thinking in us and expressing himself freely through us, and we must face up to the fact that all such things must be cut off altogether out of our lives. We dare not touch or use them any longer.

There are five things which I have found in my own experience to be like keys to victory and which enable us to witness clearly that we are indeed Nazarites, set apart for our Master's use. And though the secret of victory lies in the thought life, the first three Nazarite locks have to do with our speech. For it is a remarkable but true fact that we cannot be delivered and freed in our thought life as long as we express in words the wrong kind of thoughts.

The simple fact of saying something, has the effect of binding that thing in our thoughts. I have found that it is no use to pray to be kept from thinking wrongly unless at the same time I am willing to have all my words censored by the Holy Spirit. But as soon as I agree with him that never again am I to say a single thing which is not in harmony with the law of holy love, and the first time I begin to practice this by refusing to utter the wrong kind of word or sentence—that moment the thought victory begins. And every refusal and thrusting back of the wrong speaking, means deliverance from the wrong thinking.

The first Nazarite lock, therefore, is the vow that by God's grace and power, we will never again utter a criticizing or disparaging or unkind or unloving remark about anyone else.

In my own case the habit of fault-finding and hurrying to point out the blemishes and weaknesses in others had been so terribly strong, that I felt quite certain this was one of the first things which must go if holy love was to be free to use my mouth. I also felt equally certain that the habit was so fixed and so powerful that I never would be able to stop indulging it. I might, with a great effort, remember sometimes, but it seemed quite certain I could never be free from it. What! never again express a critical, unkind, disparaging word against anyone—the cranky, exasperating, spiteful and unloving people as well as the saints! And never gossip again, or enjoy the pleasure of passing on some unsavory little tidbit about a neighbor or someone I disliked!

Well, that would mean I must not listen to it either if I could possibly avoid doing so, for I certainly would not be able to keep it to myself if I heard an exciting but unsavory piece of news connected with a neighbor! Forego all the ugly pleasure of tearing some unpleasant person to pieces behind their back and of warning someone who had not yet discovered the unpleasant trait in that person for themselves! Never get all the exasperation and irritation and dislike and resentment off my chest by unloading it on to a friend and pouring out all the wrongs I had to bear, and forego the necessary sympathy! Indeed, it did look utterly impossible!

But, like everything else, I made the discovery that if we are willing to make a clean sweep without any reservations or exceptions, then the Savior will gladly give full victory. It is the reservations and the exceptions we insist on making which spell failure and disaster. Willingness to go the whole way and to agree that there shall be no exceptions to grieve the Holy Spirit of love, this is the secret of victory. No exceptions whatever!

When one begins to experience the glory and release which follows, the very thought of returning to the old kind of destructive and unloving thoughts and speech, becomes a kind of nightmare; quite literally, like moving out of heaven with all its radiant and loving fellowship into an atmosphere which by contrast seems like the outskirts of hell (which, indeed, I believe it really is).

This first key is so important I think I really must reiterate and reemphasize the fact that thought the victory and transformation take place in our thought life, there can be no victory and no transformation there unless our mouths and speech are included. For the interplay and connection between thought and some expression of the thought is so inseparable, that every expression by word of mouth impresses the thought more deeply on the mind, so that one simply cannot stop thinking about the things one speaks about.

We retain in our memories and consciousness the things which we talk about to others, and indeed, every time we mention a thing, we impress it more vividly upon our consciousness. That is why we find that we cannot forgive and forget any wrong done to us, as long as we talk about it to others, even in the strictest confidence. We bind the wrong that has been done to us upon our memories and consciousness and can never go free from the resultant bitterness and resentment and self-pity and dislike or hate of the wrongdoer.

To forgive and to obtain release from an unforgiving spirit, we must cut off completely all talking about the thing which has been done against us. Indeed, if we continue to talk about it and to tell others how we have been mistreated, we are not forgiving, and consequently (as our Lord tells us), we cannot be forgiven either. It seems hardly possible to overemphasize this tremendously important truth, because so many sincere Christians seem unaware of it.

If, therefore, we sincerely long to be delivered from wrong habits of thought, we must agree at the same time to be delivered from wrong habits of speech, for the two things go together. Undoubtedly, even gossip and careless chatter about the idiosyncracies and weaknesses of others makes a transformed thought life impossible. On such apparently small and trivial things do great inner revolutions and victories depend! And think of the glory of the result, the exquisite, the rapturous liberty that follows, to be free for ever of having to say or think unheavenly, unloving and unlovely things. It is paradise itself!

I do know, of course, that those who are responsible for the training of children and young people, and those who have to give references and report on those under their care and training, are in a different category; for it is doing a great wrong and injury to another person to withhold one's true knowledge of a person's character and weaknesses and temptations under those circumstances. Many a tragedy on the mission field has resulted from the sending forth of individuals who were utterly unsuited in character and Christian development for such work, simply because the referees were too loving or too weak to wish to tell the difficult truth.

Those who are asked to give references must, in justice to those who inquire, give their true judgment and not hide unpalatable facts. How much more then than any other people do such responsible seniors need to be filled with the Holy Spirit of love and to allow him to think his thoughts in them in connection with such heart searching and responsible and painful work. And how carefully we should all avoid expressing any such judgments and criticisms unnecessarily and to people not concerned in the matter.

Also, if we really desire a transformed thought life, it will be equally necessary to avoid always, and without exception, drawing the attention of others to our own supposed merits, usefulness and Christian witness. Especially to avoid sharing on every possible occasion the opportunities which we have had for personal work, or the results achieved through our messages at meetings or in other ways. Self-display can be a terribly subtle thing and can be so easily disguised from ourselves by imagining that we are only talking about these things, and the way that God has used us, in order that he may be glorified. But so often the real reason is that others may know how we are used.

It may well occur to the reader at this point to wonder what difference there is between witnessing to the saving and delivering power of Christ and the victory that he can give, without at the same time falling into the snare of self-display by claiming that we are experiencing it in daily victory, and are more victorious in Christian living than others! It is indeed important to be conscious of this subtle danger.

But at the same time it is possible to share with others and to witness to the grace and love and gentleness and power of the Savior without at the same time drawing attention to our own supposed rather special obedience and sacrifice and fruitfulness! Those who know the secret of wherein their only strength lies, may gladly share the secret with others who long to know it too, but let us beware of interweaving into that witness an account of the unusual devotion and response on our part, or the fruit which we imagine to be the result.

An illustration may help to make this clearer. A man may quite legitimately share with his friends the fact that he has just been left an inheritance which enables him to change his whole way of living, and there is no self-display in that. But supposing every time he meets you afterward he is bursting with news of how he gave a gift to help so-and-so, and lent a helping hand to another by giving him a loan, and gave old so-and-so the first good holiday he had ever had, and Aunt Matilda the fur coat she had wanted for years.

All this could be shared in a hearty and happy manner, under the guise of letting our friends know what a great deal of good a legacy can do, especially if it falls into the hands of someone who likes to be generous! But all the same, it is likely we would soon be suspecting that the hearty, careless manner was really an expression of self-display and was meant to impress on us the fact that it was a good thing the inheritance had been left to such a fine person and one who would use it so unselfishly.

We need to let the Holy Spirit of truth and love search us very carefully every time we witness to the power of Christ and the joy and satisfaction of being in his service, so that we are not found rushing to make sure that everybody knows all the details of how he has used us day by day. How often we tell ourselves that it is only for God's glory that we mention the opportunity we had to speak with someone, or to lead them to Christ; or to refer to blessing resulting from messages that we have given at meetings. But it is all too possible that we are really much more anxious that our friends and everybody else should realize how we have been used by God.

My own painful experience is that as long as I speak about my own fruit and victories and the way I am used and the opportunities I have, I cannot know thought victory, but am shut up to thinking about myself and my concerns and to daydreaming about the way in which God uses me. And that is not heaven, it is the pleasant, flowery path towards a condition in which a person can only be interested in themselves. Alas! how many a great and gifted Christian has been snared into imprisoning themselves into a thought life in which they could do nothing but let their thoughts revolve around themselves and their successes and popularity and triumphs. There is no bondage more dreary and more un-heaven-like than this.

And what bitterness and jealousy and inner rage ensues when someone comes along who is more popular and more sought after or has bigger and better placards and advertisements. No, if we want to live in heaven and know the liberty and joy and peace and delight of that kingdom of love becoming real in our thought life, there can be no talking about our own victories and fruitfulness and opportunities. It can be done (even for years) and leave us apparently fine Christians to outward appearance, but anyone who does it cannot know at the same time the glory of a transformed thought life, nor the victory of having every thought brought into captivity to Christ. The two things cannot go together. We must choose one or the other.

The third Nazarite lock also has to do with our mouths as well as our thoughts. It is the vow that all grumbling and discontented talk must cease. This becomes quite obvious when we remember that we are to go through each day praising for everything! Naturally there will be nothing to grumble, murmur or moan about, because all things will become opportunities for reacting with praise and creative power, changing the bad and upsetting things into material out of which to develop trust or submission, confidence and faith, or patience and gentleness or any other reaction which is indicated by the Spirit of holy love.

Even if it should be some great frustration or disappointment and appear to be due entirely to the machinations of the enemy, there need be no grumbling or complaint. That was the miserable, destructive and un-creative way in which the children of Israel reacted to the tests and trials in the wilderness. They were a nation of grumblers and could produce nothing acceptable to God.

It is always a help to remind ourselves that whatever the frustrating or overwhelming happening may be, there are only two possible reasons for its occurrence—either we ourselves were in danger or making a mistake, and God has intervened in this way to prevent it and to lead us into a still more blessed experience of victory and fruitfulness; or else the hindrance was manufactured by the enemy. In that case, if we trust and react peacefully, we shall have another glorious opportunity of seeing the enemy put to confusion and his plans thwarted and overthrown. So whichever it is, there really is nothing to moan about, but everything to praise for!

If this is the case in the big testings of life, how much more ought we to react with praise to every small test and disappointment, even, for instance, to such things as the weather. Why should a child of God who has the unutterable privilege of living in heaven, be heard grumbling about the weather on earth? We need to remember that small, insignificant and apparently harmless grumbles can, and do, act as tiny punctures through which all the power which the Savior offers us, leaks away.

Many a child of God who begins to check up on this matter will be astonished to discover how negative and complaining their thoughts and words are about a multitude of things, and how habitual this habit of grumbling has become, though they have been nearly unconscious of it.

We shall find, too, when once we face this matter, that every new test and trial which we meet is really the beginning (as the psalmist expresses it) of "learning a new song of praise unto our God." So let us make sure that the opening bars of the new song are not a dirge, nor a moan, nor a sigh, or the whole song will be spoiled and the learning of it be painful and not joyous.

The fourth and fifth points which concern our imaginations and our reading habits are so important they must each have a separate chapter.

CHAPTER 7
Gift of Imagination

"*And God saw that the wickedness of man was great in the earth and that every imagination of the thoughts of his heart was only evil continually*" (*Gen. 6:5*).

"*And thou, Solomon my son, know the God of thy father and serve him with a perfect heart and with a willing mind: for the Lord searcheth all hearts, and understandeth all the imaginations of the thoughts: if thou seek him, he will be found of thee, but if thou forsake him, he will cast thee off*" (*1 Chron. 28:9*).

The fourth Nazarite vow concerns the use which we make of our imaginations. Many of us who have suffered from overly vivid imaginations are inclined to think that this faculty is the greatest of all snares. That is because we have fallen into the habit of using it in completely wrong ways just as had the people described in Genesis 6:5. People who are martyrs to anxieties and fears of all kinds will find that their misuse of their imaginations is the root cause of the trouble. They just cannot stop picturing all the dreadful and overwhelming and unbearable things which may happen in the future; and every event to which they look forward with dread, they picture over and over again, along with their future reactions to it, until they are nervous wrecks.

But other people misuse their imaginations just as badly. If they are specially gifted, successful, and popular people (or if they are just the opposite and need to compensate themselves), how often they use this private cinema show which we all possess, to throw on the screen of their imagination a whole series of pictures in which they are the central figure around whom everything revolves. How liable we all are to make ourselves the heroes and heroines of all our inner imaginings! This is what makes us such selfish and irritable and disagreeable people to live with. We are always imagining how we want other people to act, and we expect them to behave in the way which we have pictured and which gratifies us. And when they don't and won't, we resent it!

Over and over again in the Old Testament we read of the children of Israel burning incense to idols. And what is this misuse of our imaginations: This habit of throwing ourselves on the screen of our minds in the form of charming and delightful gods and goddesses to whom everyone must render admiration and homage and do as we desire? What is this but the very same idolatry and burning of incense to ourselves? We shall never know the glory and joy of a transformed thought life until the Savior delivers us completely from this degrading habit of daydreaming about ourselves.

But having said all that, the truth remains that the imagination is the greatest and most creative and God-like function which our Father in heaven has bestowed upon us. And if only we would allow the Holy Spirit of love to teach us how to use it, how enormously enriched our lives would be.

I think it is a safe rule that we are never meant to use our imaginations in order to picture ourselves in the chief role. Never. The center of interest in the pictures created in our minds must never be ourselves. But how unspeakably valuable this wonderful power is in enabling us to put ourselves in the place of other people so that we may be able to feel with them and understand their situation as could never otherwise be the case.

83

Then what a wonderful asset to prayer the imagination is, enabling us to go and stand alongside those we are praying for, almost as though we were conversing with them face to face. How the ability to picture our loved ones and bring them before us enhances the joy and blessedness of prayer, and kindles love and sympathy and desire to help.

We can even picture the mission fields of the world although we have never visited them in person. But the news and descriptions which we have heard from missionaries home on furlough, and the books we have read, all provide material out of which this wonderful and God-like ability to imagine can create and bring before us scenes and needs which call forth prayer and desire in our hearts in the most remarkable and lovely way.

Alexander Whyte has rightly and wonderfully described this greatest of all gifts which God has given us. He says of the imagination: "It makes us full of eyes, without and within." The imagination is far stronger than any other power which we possess, and the psychologists tell us that on occasions, when the will and the imagination are in conflict, the imagination always wins.

How important therefore that we should vow by the Savior's help never to throw the wrong kind of pictures on this screen in our minds for the imagination literally has the power of making the things we picture real and effective. Every worrier and every person tormented with fear, knows this only too well. Never picture anything you are afraid of, or the fear will become more real than reality itself.

But, personally, I believe that the noblest and most glorious and most blessed function of the imagination is to make it possible for the invisible and eternal things to become real to us.

Multitudes of Christians who sadly confess that the Lord Jesus seems so unreal to them and so far away and vague that they never feel any vital contact with him, would find that he has provided for this very difficulty, and our imagination is the remedy. If we would but picture him as vividly and clearly as possible as he is revealed to us in the Gospels, as he was away there in Galilee and in Jerusalem and Judea, and if we spoke to him as we would if we actually saw him under those conditions, we would find all the unreality vanish away. Some people are honestly terrified of using their imaginations in connection with their faith in the Savior.

I once said to a Christian friend, "Whenever I have a quiet time and whenever I pray, I imagine the Lord Jesus himself close beside me, and then I speak to him as if I saw him face to face. That makes it easy to talk to him as naturally and simply as I would if I really could see him."

She answered, almost with horror, "Oh,

but it is very dangerous to imagine things. Imaginary things are not real, we make them up ourselves."

But of course, when we pray we do nothing of the kind. For nothing is more sure and more attested to in the Scriptures than the fact that our Lord is actually present with us in some lovely and mysterious way and, therefore, we are meant to behave and to speak exactly as we would if we could see him. We do not try to make him present and real when we use our imagination, because he really is there, and when we happily and thankfully use this God-given faculty it simply makes the wonderful truth more real to us—though not, of course, to him.

Half the time those people who complain that spiritual things are so unreal to them and that they cannot realize the Lord's presence, do not understand this is simply and solely because they are afraid to accept and believe the glorious truth told us in the Bible and attested to by innumerable Christian witnesses, that the Lord really is present with his people.

Nobody could pray drearily or despairingly or indifferently to their Savior, or think of him as unreal, if they saw him close beside them; and through the eyes of our imagination we may see him, vividly and gloriously present. For an imagination used as God means it to be used, in order to visualize true things described to us in the

Scriptures, does indeed make a soul full of eyes within and without.

Let us take a simple illustration. Suppose you are parted from your best friend, or your lover, at different ends of the country, and you arrange to speak to each other over the telephone every morning and evening at a certain time. Now, when you pick up the telephone receiver, you cannot see the one you are so longing to speak to, but on such occasions, instinctively and rejoicingly, you use the lovely gift of creative imagination which God has given you, and you imagine the one that you are going to talk to exactly in the form which you know and love so well. Then the conversation is as easy and natural and spontaneous and delightful as though you were actually speaking face to face.

If, however, you are silly and absurd enough as to misuse your imagination and deliberately picture to yourself some utterly different person at the other end of the line, perhaps some pompous, overwhelming person with a forbidding frown or an angry expression, how strained and artificial and false and unpleasant the whole conversation is likely to be.

In the four Gospels we have a most beautifully true and lifelike portrait of our Lord and Savior and Redeemer, Jesus Christ; not, certainly, of his personal appearance, but of himself, his character, his reactions to every conceivable circumstance and person. We know exactly what he is like with sinners, with suffering and sorrowful people, with hypocrites and self-righteous Pharisees, and with the needy and distressed and lonely. We see him pictured among those who loved him and longed to serve and to please him; and we see him among the unclean and the outcast whom nobody else loved.

Then all we have to do is to study this lovely portrait of him continually, and when we pray picture to ourselves this one who has revealed himself so intimately and fully as the lover of all men. I, myself, see no harm but rather find immense help, in picturing, too, the kind of face and expression such an one would have, the strongest, bravest, gentlest, kindest, most understanding and most challenging face that I can imagine.

I know, of course, that this imagined picture will not be, and cannot be, anything as wonderful as the reality. I do the best I can, however, and imagine the face of that one turned toward me, seeing me just as I am, sin-stained or cleansed, sad or happy, tempest-tossed or delivered, assailed by temptation, fallen and defiled, or risen and washed and made holy again. When I am anxious and terrified I picture him as present; and also when I am bursting with thankfulness and relief because of some wonderful deliverance he has wrought for me, or for some abundant supply to a special need. There is no difficulty, then, in loving that Savior, and no real impossibility in realizing his presence.

In this connection it is very interesting to notice that although the Lord Jesus said to his disciples, "When ye pray say, Our Father which art in heaven," in actual fact, after the resurrection, there is not one single recorded prayer in which God is so addressed. In the Acts of the Apostles every prayer recorded is addressed to the Lord whom the Apostles and early Christians identified with the Lord Jesus exactly as though he were visible present amongst them. (See Acts 1:24; 4:24; 4:29; 7:55, 59, 60; 9:10, 13; 10:4; 16:10; 18:9.)

Of course the Epistles are full of references to God the Father of the Lord Jesus and of us all, but to the early Christians it seemed that he had come so close to them and made himself so accessible to them in the incarnation in Jesus Christ that in all their prayers they spoke direct to the Lord Jesus himself, who, during the forty days between his resurrection and his ascension, had taught them this wonderful lesson: "Lo, I am with you alway."

They had learned this by experience and in a most beautiful way. For sometimes during those forty days he was visible to them, but more often invisible. Then, when he appeared in their midst again they found that he had heard and seen all that they had said and done when they had supposed him to be absent because he had been invisible. No wonder that after those forty days they continued to speak to him as though they saw him and acted as though they were in his presence all the time.

Surely this is the blessed and unique secret which all Christians need to learn, and which, when learned, entirely transforms our life on earth. For when we realize this fact, then we know that we face nothing alone, neither temptation, test or trial, and that nothing can separate us from the presence and love of Christ or from contact with his power.

Mother Julian, who lived in the fourteenth century, shares with us her own lovely experience in this matter. She says: "He willeth that we believe that we see him continually . . . and in this belief he maketh us evermore to gain grace. For he will be seen and he will be sought: he will be abided and he will be trusted . . . For of all things the beholding and the loving of the Maker maketh the soul to seem least in his own sight, and most filleth it with true meekness; with plenty of charity to his even-Christians" (fellow Christians).

We see, then, that if we habitually misuse our imaginations and picture unclean and distorted and hateful things, we shall need to allow the Savior to cleanse and thoroughly transform this most creative of all our faculties so that the kingdom of heaven and all its joy and glory of love can become real in our thought life.

Then let us not be afraid to use this God-given power which makes us full of eyes so that all heaven and its glories begin to open before us. Only let us be filled with fear and loathing at the very thought of continuing to use it in any wrong or impure way, for "Blessed are the pure in heart (thought) for they shall see God."

This brings us to another point which is of great importance, for it is vitally linked up with the imagination. Just as we find that we have no power to think the right kind of thoughts until our speech is also brought under the control of the Holy Spirit of love, so in the same way we shall find that we have no power to change our wrong imaginings or to be free from the habit of daydreaming about ourselves until we allow the Holy Spirit to control our reading habits.

It is really striking how the inner and outer victories depend upon one another. The eyes of our imagination will never become cleansed and pure until the eyes of our body are also cleansed. So much depends upon what we look at and what we read, and in modern life so many of the things which we read (with their accompanying illustrations) can be a real cause of failure by continually stimulating the imagination in the wrong way. But this is the subject of the next chapter.

CHAPTER 8
Challenge to Our Reading Habits

"... There is a great deal we should like to say about this ... but it is not easy to explain to you since you seem so slow to grasp spiritual truth ... Anyone who continues to live on milk is obviously immature, he simply has not grown up. Solid food is only for the adult, that is for the man who has developed by his experience, his power to discriminate between what is good and bad for him ... Cannot we leave spiritual babyhood behind and go on to maturity?" (Heb. 5:11, 13-14)

I do realize that although the subject of this chapter, our reading habits, is an intensely important one for all Christians, our Lord does not lead all his children to exactly the same conclusions, and that what proves harmful to some may be perfectly wholesome and good for others. Indeed, I think it very possible that some unimaginative people who tend to rather narrow ideas, might find themselves greatly enriched and benefited by reading in moderation just the kind of books which I have had to lay aside altogether just because they proved a snare to me personally, because I could not enjoy them in moderation.

Being a very imaginative person, I have found that if my imagination is to remain holy and healthy and happy and utterly at the disposal of the Holy Spirit, and be creative in the way he means it to be, then I must never allow it to be stimulated by the wrong kind of literature. Just as speech and thinking go together, so reading and imagination go together, and I found that it was absolutely essential that I should cut off the wrong kind of reading just as drastically as I was to cut out all criticizing of others and all boasting and all grumbling. It was quite clear, and there has had to be a complete and glorious revolution in my reading habits.

For me, this fifth Nazarite vow was almost like plucking out my own right eye, for being a very imaginative person, all my own tastes lay in the direction of highly imaginative, sensational and romantic literature. I was a most voracious reader of good novels, adventure tales, detective tales and stories in illustrated magazines. And I can only say when I was confronted by the fact that this was one of the chief causes of my unruly and unclean imagination (because I always substituted myself for the heroine in the story and added a great deal of highly colored episodes undreamed of by the author), it was a real shock.

For though I saw plainly that such reading did feed and stimulate my imagination in the wrong way, yet it did seem to me that a most forbidding, drab and dismal future lay ahead of me if I made this vow. For apparently all the literature which I was accustomed to read for pleasure and relaxation and which (as I had rationalized it to myself) kept me normal and in touch with real life, must from then on be resolutely rejected. I had always looked upon such reading as a passionate necessity, both as a way of escape from drab surroundings and as a legitimate relaxation.

At the same time I did know that I was not the sort of person who could indulge moderately in such reading, any more than some people can drink in moderation. In my case it was an inordinate affection, and when I was immersed in a thrilling book woe betide the person who interrupted me or wanted help from me. It was even difficult to lay aside the book in order to talk to some visitor seeking spiritual help, but—and this is significant—in those days there were not many who did seek such help!

I told myself that people ought not to come bothering me during my free time, just when I really needed to relax and get away from my work. It makes me almost tremble now when I remember the ungracious, indeed, rude and unwilling-to-be-disturbed attitude which this inordinate love of reading the world's literature had ingrained in my character.

Yes, an exceedingly ugly and un-Christian manner was the result of this wrong habit of reading, and yet, when the Holy Spirit of love brought it to my consciousness in this way, I really did not see how it was going to be possible to break free from it.

Once again, however, he showed me that victory depended on cutting off the harmful habit altogether and making no exceptions. Before going any further I do want to repeat what was said at the beginning of the chapter. I am sharing with you the course which I, personally, was led to take, and I write from the standpoint of an addict who could not indulge in moderation. But I would like to suggest in passing that for some Christians such a course might be most undesirable. Some people would be greatly enriched if they did sometimes read books which would stimulate their almost dormant imaginations, and there is plenty of the right sort of fiction which would help them in this way.

On the other hand, there are different kinds of addiction! Some Christians tend to have one track minds and it is astonishing how many become absorbed in one special aspect of religious truth or one special subject in the Bible, and who tend more and more to read only such books as deal with that special subject. It is possible to tell oneself that we are becoming experts in that important matter which other Christians have ignored.

Quite possibly, however, we are only becoming lopsided, and it might be a most wholesome thing, to cut off completely for some months all further reading on that one special topic which now absorbs (perhaps even wastes) too much of our time. To embark upon a completely different course of reading might well prove an almost startlingly enriching experience. I am dearly tempted to list a few of those special subjects on which some earnest Christians tend to become addicts so that they can scarcely enjoy reading about anything else—but I will not do so!

It is enough to warn any fellow Christian who, like myself, cannot graciously lay aside a thrilling book of fiction, and who spend nearly all their spare time (and often more than their spare time!) lost in such reading, that we are addicts! Like those who cannot drink in moderation, our safest plan is to cut it off altogether. For me it meant a clean sweep, for a time at least, of all fiction and of all secular magazines. But I never for a moment suspected it would open to me a new world of knowledge and joy and power and delight, and prove to be one of the most enriching decisions which the Lord has ever led me to take.

Some time ago I received a letter from a friend who had just been reading *The Kingdom of Love*, and had come across the paragraph in which I referred briefly to the way in which I had been led to alter my reading habits. She wrote something like this:

"I cannot help feeling that it is a great pity that you have decided to cut your reading so drastically. When I was a young Christian I also felt very strongly on this matter and restricted my reading in the same way, and now I cannot help deeply regretting the fact, as I find myself terribly ignorant of many matters and points of view which I ought to know about, and I feel that as a result my life has been greatly and irretrievably impoverished."

When I first read this lovingly intended warning, I could not help smiling a little, for the result from the changes in my own reading, so far from destroying and narrowing my reading, has been the means of bringing me more enrichment than almost anything else in my life. It has opened up to me so many new and helpful and suggestive points of view that I am almost overwhelmed with astonishment and horror as I look back on the dreary, narrow, completely uninspiring diet of fiction and illustrated magazines on which I had so largely fed my mind.

I also quickly realized that my friend's fear was grounded in a misapprehension of my meaning, and in the paragraph referred to I had not stated the facts sufficiently clearly. For mine had been a most terribly wasteful way of enjoying the pleasures of reading. Whenever I was free I scanned the book-shelves and tables of my friends for something light and easy to relax with. By this I meant something which need not greatly stimulate my mind to thought, but only stimulate my imagination to dream!

Of course, I read a few other books as well —travel stories, biographies and autobiographies and some well written missionary books, but my first choice for all spare moments was an illustrated magazine, a Wodehouse or a *Punch*, a thriller or detective story, or a romance. Sordid and ugly and distorted books emphasizing abnormal and perverted phases of life did not appeal to me; I liked books with happy endings and about nice people, but if they did not turn out to be nice people I still read the book.

If you are surprised at such a preference on the part of an earnest missionary, I can only say that a good many other equally earnest missionaries have the same idea and the same taste, and we can give you very plausible reasons for it! Such as:

"We have been hectically busy for hours in

sordid, ugly surroundings, with sick, or difficult, or desperately ignorant people. We are tired and strained and things tend to get on our nerves, and now we need to relax and to get back to normal as soon as possible. Our tired brains feel just like wet rags and will not allow us to concentrate on anything which needs special or careful thought in order to take it in. And here, in this magazine or this novel, is the ideal way by which to escape quickly and harmlessly for an hour or two, right out of the strain and stress of our environment, into a different scene altogether and with no effort on our part at all.

"Then, too, we have seen so many unfortunate results in the lives of the very narrow people who refuse to read anything which does not coincide with their own dogmatic point of view or the ideas among which they grew up. We see examples all the time of how cranky and odd and difficult to live and work with such people can become, indeed, sometimes quite unbalanced. And we prefer to keep as sane and sensible and ordinary as possible by reading books which deal with ordinary life and not just with missionary and religious problems. We need, also, to keep in touch with the point of view of the people around us, even if it is a worldly point of view."

This was my own former attitude, but now I am firmly convinced that there is a far better way! Certainly the interesting, exciting, non-thought-provoking books which I used to read for relaxation did have the effect of helping me to forget the irritating outer world and to feel less strained for an hour or two. But they had absolutely no creative, healing or strengthening effect upon me.

They did not make me fitter and stronger or more patient in preparation for the battle ahead, nor for the next day's work. Neither did they relax me in such a way that I should not feel so tired and exhausted in the future, for they did not introduce me to a higher plane of spiritual life and energy where I could renew my strength in such a way that my body and nerves would be quickened and charged with a new life.

They did help me temporarily to forget the tiredness and the vexations of the moment. But (and this is the important part), they made me waste the time which might have been spent reading quite a different kind of literature which would have had a completely different effect upon me, namely books written by writers who knew the secret of how to retire into a far more real and beautiful world where higher powers and quickening energies can be contacted, and where one can, as it were, bathe in a fountain of light and life and love; returning afterwards to the daily duties of life, not only relaxed and rested, but gloriously stimulated, spiritually, mentally and physically and energized with a new kind of power.

You may be inclined, when you read this, to react with incredulity and to exclaim: "Impossible! What sort of literature could I get hold of which would do that to me?"

Frankly, that was my own inner feeling when the Lord told me that if I wanted to experience a thought life completely controlled and transformed by the Holy Spirit of love, and if I wanted to live in the healing and strengthening atmosphere of the heavenly places, I must completely revolutionize my reading habits. Of course, I found he was absolutely right! And now I must tell you of the extraordinary discovery I made and its revolutionary results.

The first step, of course, was to alter my principle of selection completely, it so happens that for several years now my work has kept me traveling the whole time, in many different countries, and seldom spending more than a few weeks in any one place. This means that I cannot join a library, nor choose books which I particularly wish to read.

On the other hand I receive a great deal of wonderful hospitality in the homes of God's people, and their bookcases are just as hospitably set before me. On approaching those bookcases I now exercise an entirely new principle of selection, and search them with a surge of excitement, hope and delighted expectation never before imagined. What new treasure which I have never before had the opportunity to read has the Lord provided for me on these shelves? What new window looking into heaven will be set open before me? Or what new and unexpected pathway shall I follow leading out into a whole realm of glorious experience never known before?

The hours which would once have been wasted on fiction and secular topics are now filled with spiritual discoveries and adventures more delightful and more wonderful and entrancing than anything I had ever before imagined.

Of course, it is true that people's bookshelves vary very greatly! But that adds to the interest and excitement, for I never know what I shall find. It is not by any means upon all bookshelves that one finds volumes with this glorious power of opening doors and windows into new realms of the spirit.

In practically every home, without exception (except those where no books are to be found at all) I have spent many happy and deeply interesting hours reading books dealing with a wide field of subjects on which I had been largely or totally ignorant. In some homes, where other fare was not provided, I have very usefully polished my knowledge on my particularly weak subjects. Indeed, in one place where the room allotted to me contained nothing but discarded school books and adventure stories, I spent some fascinating hours studying a primary book on Algebra, a subject I had never been able to make head or tail of at school, and which I now discovered with pleasure, was not so incomprehensible as I had always supposed.

But—and this is the great point—how often the shelves have yielded absolutely priceless treasures, books written by almost unknown or forgotten Christians of the past, by the great saints of every age and every school of thought and every section of the Church. Books which even their owners had never read or whose existence they had forgotten about. Books by men and women who had become experts in spiritual things and who had been led to share their experiences and their discoveries with others. Writers, who, if they could not tell me all the things I longed to know, could point me to signposts along the way and to paths which, when explored, led me out into completely new realms of understanding.

Sometimes, after pressing through thickets of theories, I would find myself led to a place from which I beheld a vista of new aspects of the truth more beautiful than can be described.

It does, indeed, seem that the Lord loves to help and illumine us through the shared experiences and discoveries of his people, though they come from the most diverse environments and background. The explorations and findings of the saints in all ages are for the enrichment of all who follow.

This, then, is the new principle of selection which I now practice when I approach any bookshelves, which of these books is most likely to increase my knowledge of the Lord and to strengthen my love for him?

Any writer who appears to love the Lord Jesus passionately, and who seems just as passionately desirous that we should love him too, that is the writer I choose. I ask with eager hope, "Will this book give news of the wonderful ways in which he teaches his people, and supports and strengthens them under testings and fiery trials? Are there vital lessons which he has taught the writer of this book about which I am still in complete or partial ignorance? Shall I learn here some new and practical way in which I can respond to him more fully? Am I going to love him more, after reading this book, and am I going to long more passionately for others to love and know him too?"

If, as I dip into the book and skim through the pages, it appears likely that it really will have this heartwarming effect, then I carry it off as hopefully as a miner who thinks he has struck a vein of gold, and quite regardless of what school of thought the writer may belong to.

Do I ever read books by authors differing in their teaching from the particular school of thought in which I was nurtured and trained? Yes, I must confess that I do if the book appears likely to contain the kind of matter which I have described, and that for two reasons.

First, I am now firmly convinced that

sometimes writers are labeled as dangerous or unsound absolutely unjustly, simply because they are looking at some truth from a different angle to the one from which we are accustomed to look at it. They therefore see some aspects hitherto hidden from us; or they have penetrated further into that truth than we have and see things beyond our own narrow point of view.

Sometimes also because, in their eager desire to help others to see more clearly, they use a different phraseology or idiom to the one we have become accustomed to, so that perhaps we may be startled into looking more closely into the meaning of phrases and words and quotations from the Bible which we have heard so often that our response to them is in danger of being blunted. All too often we slap some adverse label on to an author merely on the report of some confirmed heresy-hunter who zealously spends the time in ferreting out error instead of searching for long mislaid nuggets of truth.

A real heresy-hunter is bound to be blinded and prejudiced, for nothing is easier than to find error where no error is, if you are zealously looking for it and are going to take words out of their context. In scientific search and experiment all sorts of false paths are followed and proved wrong, but even so the experimenters may stumble across some fact which is new and absolutely relevant and which may be a further link or clue pointing others toward the truth and the real solution and answer to the problem which they are all investigating. So, in our longing for deeper insight into the truth, the Holy Spirit may often give us vital light through some writer with whom we absolutely disagree on other points.

But there is a second reason for reading books from quite another point of view to one's own. I frankly confess that I sometimes continue to read right through a book in which I find many things which I firmly believe to be errors and false clues or trials, things in which the writer really seems to be mistaken and deceived. It is possible there may be other things in the book which throw vivid and lovely light on passages in the Bible or experiences of life which before had greatly perplexed me. Then I feel with great thankfulness that it will be worthwhile to read through to the end, discarding all that I cannot agree with and gratefully assimilating all that does enrich my understanding and by which the Holy Spirit illumines me.

It may be objected at this point that where there is obvious error, everything else must be suspect. But surely nothing can be further from the truth! Everybody is mistaken in some things, and ignorant of many other things because they have not yet had opportunity to learn about subjects on which others may be experts. But it is pretty safe to say that everybody we meet knows something which we do not, and this principle holds good in Christian experience and understanding also.

This is a vital point which all Christians should frankly acknowledge to themselves, namely if we are going to insist that because a man preaches, teaches or writes some things which we are convinced are untrue and even dangerous distortions of the truth, therefore everything which that man teaches, preaches and writes is tainted with error and must not be read or listened to; then on the same principle we cannot expect other people to read or listen to our own exposition of the truth, but they too must repudiate all that we teach or write. For nothing is clearer than the fact that there is some error and distortion of the truth in every school of thought and among all sections of the Christian Church.

No one group has nothing but pure doctrine, all are mixed with error. And no one group has all the truth, but in every group there will be found at least a modicum of some truth which the other groups have overlaid, or mislaid, or fail to emphasize. The thing which we need to learn above all others is, not to repudiate everything which is mixed with error, but how to bring forth the precious from the vile, and how to know and recognize truth wherever we find it, in the most unlikely places, and to treasure it and add it to our store of knowledge.

I do believe that the enemy of our souls

and minds has been quite fiendishly skillful in persuading many earnest and devout Christians that they must repudiate altogether everything which is not found in their own school of thought, instead of humbly and fearlessly allowing the Holy Spirit to make us skillful in discerning between true and untrue. It is only thus we may be led into fuller truth through the contributions of other groups of Christians. The writer to the Hebrews seems to have felt this very strongly:

"There is a great deal which we would like to say to you . . . but it is not easy since you seem so slow to grasp spiritual truth. At a time when you should be teaching others, you need teachers yourselves to repeat to you the ABC of God's revelation to men! Anyone who continues to live on milk is obviously immature, he simply has not grown up. Solid food is only for the adult, that is, for the man who has developed by experience his power to discriminate between what is good and what is bad for him. Let us leave behind the elementary teaching about Christ and go forward to adult understanding. Let us not lay over and over again the foundation truths. No, if God allows, let us go on" (Heb. 5:11—6:1, Phillips).

At this point, however, we need to look at a very important objection and warning. Is it not dangerous to set the example of reading books which contain a mixture of truth and error, for fear of encouraging young Christians and converts to do so too, and thereby leading them into danger before they are spiritually mature enough to discern which is truth and which is only alluring error?

This is indeed a most important point. But once again there is an equally important thing to be emphasized. The teachings and writings of all Christians, even those who profess to contain the purest doctrine, do all contain a mixture of truth and error, and therefore, we would have to warn young Christians and converts against reading the books of even the writers we are most sure of. For this must be the case if we insist on the principle of repudiating all teaching which is not pure truth.

At the same time it is most important that they should not be led into any kind of error or danger, and that they should be encouraged from the very beginning to read and study books which will ground them firmly and strongly in the glorious truths so dear to us and of such priceless value. They cannot, however, long be protected from coming up against errors and speculations and suggested doubts, nor are they likely to remain out of contact with people who will try to interest them in different isms.

Instead of trying to teach them all the answers to these different distortions of the truth, is it not much wiser and likely to be far more effective if we seek to ground them from the very beginning in a love for all books which strengthen their devotion to

Christ and their passion to serve him, and awaken a desire for fuller consecration to their Lord and Savior; books through the reading of which the Holy Spirit will be able to open their eyes to recognize truth wherever it may be found, in the writings of the saints of all ages, no matter what church they belonged to. Surely it is far more important to recognize truth amid a mass of error, like a priceless jewel buried in clay, than to incite them to go about hunting for error.

A miner in a gold mine looks for the gold, not for useless or spurious ore, and joyfully digs it out embedded in a mass of material which is not gold. But all too often we discourage young Christians from beginning to mine for themselves and try to make them satisfied with looking at nuggets dug out by certain miners of whom we approve. Of course we all need to be taught to recognize useless ore which can contain no gold, but it is the gold itself which we need to recognize or we shall pass it by altogether and never learn to be led by the Spirit into finding truth ourselves.

If all young Christians are taught to keep the daily quiet time with their Lord, to speak to him personally and to learn to hear his voice speaking to them, then their spiritual senses will become developed. Their love to him so quickened through obedience and devotion that it is most unlikely that any false teaching which draws off love from the Lord himself will be able to make any appeal to them. They will not feel like wasting time reading heresies and isms which seem desolatingly empty of the center of all, the Lord Jesus Christ himself.

Certainly it is tragic when sharp young Christians go to liberal theological colleges and find their intellectual beliefs undermined and their faith shattered. But surely it is equally tragic to meet some who went to fundamentalist colleges and came out with their faith based on belief in certain sound doctrines and then, when they had got well into their ministry, met someone more than their match in argument who was able to undermine their faith; so that they had the shattering and overwhelming experience of finding that with the sweeping away of their intellectual beliefs their religious foundation had been taken from them also.

This can so easily happen if belief is founded upon doctrine and not upon the Person of the Lord Jesus Christ himself, alive, present and real to us, the center of our love and loyalty. Happy are all those who, going to train for Christian work and the Christian ministry, no matter what the teaching may be and what the assaults upon their intellectual beliefs, stand fast in joyful, unbroken communion with their risen Lord and Savior himself.

This personal grounding in obedient and devoted union with the Lord will, I do believe, be immeasurably strengthened and increased by reading the experiences and discoveries about him of all the saints in all the ages and in all the many different schools of thought. It is love, and not intellectual learning, which leads us on into all truth. Love is the great opener of the understanding. Those who love see more profoundly into the truths of the gospel than all their teachers who lack or come short in that vital requisite.

We are on safe ground when we encourage any Christian to read and study the writings of the great saints and lovers of the Lord, be they Protestant or Roman Catholic, mystic or theologian. If they wrote out of a burning heart of love to Christ, we shall catch fire from the same holy flame.

On the other hand, it is all too possible that, if we encourage young Christians to read the controversies and arguments of writers who know little in actual practice of the law of love, but wrangle and disparage and despise and condemn their fellow members of Christ's Body who differ from them in interpretation, and who cast anathemas upon each other, we shall be culpably introducing them to a poisonous mental atmosphere and be guilty of a greater wrong than even that of the drug addict who introduces his friends to the same poison and leads them into the same deadly slavery as himself.

I have found such amazing help and enrichment through reading books written by those aflame with love for Christ—even when part of what they say is not in agreement with the discoveries of other equally love-inspired Christians—that I cannot escape the conclusion that God loves to give light to all who love him and through all who love him, even if what they say is mixed with some error due to their environment or the general teaching of Christians in the age in which they lived.

When all the glorious discoveries of God's people are pooled, what a dazzling, radiant, heart-ravishing store of treasure is opened to us—gems and nuggets and gold, all brought into the common treasure house by individual saints from all the visible churches in all ages! Contributions from Roman Catholic saints and medieval mystics, from Reformers and Calvinists, Quakers and Methodists, High and Low Anglicans, Plymouth Brethren and Pentecostals, Salvationists, Presbyterians and Baptists and all the other groups of Christians in all lands. Not that everything they bring is to be accepted, but everything which has contributed to their love to Christ, and through that love has opened their understanding to see more of his beauty and glory.

What a list of names, the very sound of which makes the flame of love burn stronger in our own hearts. All of us have our own individual list of those through whom we have been enriched in this way. Through them and through multitudes of others, many of them humble, almost unknown folk, God has poured into the common spiritual treasury of his people different aspects and facets of the truth. How sad to remain outside the storehouse and ignorant of some of its loveliest treasures because we are afraid to look at them lest we be beguiled into some error!

One great principle on which God works has greatly comforted me in connection with this natural fear of being led into error, and the problem of why God should be willing to lead us into truth through those in whom it is mixed with error and distortion. For have we not often wondered, some of us, at the very strange way in which he seems to use and bless the ministry of those we feel he ought not to honor in this way because they teach some things which do not seem in harmony with a true interpretation of the Scriptures, and deny some things which we believe to be vital.

It seems that the principle on which he works is this: he blesses and confirms and makes fruitful all truth wherever he finds it, no matter what strange sect or individual teaches it, and he leaves the errors to work themselves out so that through their results they expose themselves quite clearly as being false, and others can avoid them.

CHAPTER 9
Royal Law
of
Love

"Jesus said . . . Thou shalt love the Lord thy God with all thy heart, and with all thy soul, and with all thy mind. This is the first and great commandment. And the second is like unto it, Thou shalt love thy neighbor as thyself. On these two commandments hang all the law and the prophets" (Matt. 22:36-39).

"If ye fulfill the royal law according to the Scriptures, Thou shalt love thy neighbor as thyself, ye do well" (Jas. 2:8).

I have already described how immensely enriched and enlightened I have been through reading books in which the great lovers of the Lord in all ages have shared their spiritual experiences and tell us of the realms of truth into which they were led by the Holy Spirit and their discoveries in those heavenly regions.

Some writers stand out above all others in their power to convey some of their own marvelous illumination to our minds and understandings, rather like gigantic mountain peaks towering up above swirling clouds of mist, or breaking through the curtain of cloud and showing us glimpses into heavenly places. To come across the writings of such men and women for the first time, and when our own understanding has been prepared by new lessons in the school of life, constitutes, sometimes, the beginning of a completely new epoch in our lives.

Such an experience came to me when for the first time I came across the writings of an author, who in very truth, made me feel as though he had opened a door through which I was led by the Holy Spirit into the kingdom of heaven. When I think of the circumstances by which I was led to read this book, and of how nearly I missed it, my thankfulness is doubled and also mixed with trembling. It happened in this way.

I was staying at the time at a Christian guest house in New Zealand, and one day, during the midday meal in the dining room, a certain member of the party, who was usually rather silent and uncommunicative, remarked quietly that he had recently read a book by an old divine named William Law. This book, so he informed us, had completely revolutionized many of his spiritual ideas and conceptions. Nobody made any remark, and he again subsided into silence without, one supposes, the faintest idea that he had just placed a piece of live dynamite in a position where, as far as one person was concerned, it could explode with the maximum effect. We left the table, however, without my having in the least realized what he had done, and I thought no more on what he had said.

That same night, however, quite contrary to my usual happy ability to sleep peacefully throughout the night in any strange bed, I woke at midnight and began to toss and turn, and to my amazement I simply could not fall asleep again. At last I turned on the light, got out of bed, and went to the one shelf of books in the room to see if they contained anything which might contribute to making me feel sleepy. Glancing through the titles I came to one which I had noticed several times and had always discarded as looking very dull, but the title was, *"Wholly for God." Selections from William Law.* "William Law?" thought I. "Surely this must be the book mentioned at the luncheon table today."

A mild curiosity to see what a rather ordinary and prosaic young man considered revolutionary, coupled with a hope that the writings of an eminent divine of two hundred years ago might be just what I was needing to produce sleepiness, decided me in my choice. I took up *Selections from William Law*, and retired to the bed again.

On closer inspection the book appeared to consist of selections from three of the author's books entitled *The Spirit of Love, The Spirit of Prayer* and *The Serious Call to a Devout Life*. I turned to the first of the three, *The Spirit of Love*, and began at chapter one.

Whereupon, almost at once, it seemed to me that a door was opened in heaven and I found myself stumbling, groping, and dazzled with glory, in a new realm of understanding altogether. My whole mind seemed illumined with a light more lovely and entrancing and satisfying than anything I had ever dreamed of. I was in a new world of thought, a world more real and glorious than anything I had known in the world of sense, and a company of the inhabitants of that kingdom of love into which William Law had unlocked the door, appeared to receive me and surround me, welcoming me with laughter, their faces shining with a great joy.

He whom I had loved and followed for so long, albeit so blindly and with such weakness and difficulty, was there also, the crowned King of Love himself, about whom I had entertained so many distorted ideas.

He was there, flaming with love as at the burning bush.

As I think back to that amazing night I am perplexed to understand just how the book made such an impression upon me, for honesty compels me to add at once that not by any means everybody appears to react to William Law in the same way! Even the editor who recently reproduced a pocket edition of the writings of William Law, for some absolutely unaccountable reason has omitted from his edition any part of *The Spirit of Love* which had this overwhelming effect upon me and which seems to me to be incomparably his most enriching work.

John Wesley, it seems, wrote to William Law reproaching him for recommending a gospel of works and not of grace. But Wesley began with *The Serious Call*, and I began with *The Spirit of Love*, and about twenty years lay between the writing of the two books.

But it is also obvious to me now that I was led by the Holy Spirit to find this book at exactly the right moment in my spiritual life and development, so that I was able to find in it the key to the realm of Christian experience for which I had been hungering and thirsting for so long.

On others (not led by the same path and at a different stage of Christian experience), the writings of William Law, I was astonished to find, appear to have no such dynamic effect! During the next few weeks I borrowed the book and urged several friends to read it. But to one the whole conception of the book seemed so revolutionary that she did not dare to read far. And another to whom I lent it, returned it almost immediately remarking, "It's no good my going on with this, I can't make head or tail of what the fellow is driving at!" But on some, evidently, it lays the same glorious spell and unlocks the same treasure house of glory.

When I went downstairs to the breakfast table the first morning, after spending a good many hours of the night in the company of William Law and all the heavenly host, I looked almost diffidently across the table at the young man I had so erroneously supposed to be dull and lacking interest. I thanked him for introducing me to the book, adding that I could not possibly begin to explain the stupendous revolution in my thinking since we had met at the table the night before. He looked at me gravely, but with perfect understanding, and said simply, "I know exactly what you mean, for I myself can never be the same again since reading it."

I have often tried to analyze just what happened in my mind on that eventful night, and how the light broke upon me, but it is not easy to do so. It was so like a sudden rending of a veil of misunderstanding and misconception that I cannot remember just what words or phrases or paragraphs in the book did it. But I do remember that some veil over my mind began to be torn aside almost from the first moment and I found myself exclaiming in dazed joy: "This—this at last is what I have been longing and searching for all my Christian life."

Then there came as it were the rent in the veil, and after that it was not words in a book any longer, but the Lord of Love himself coming to meet me in person and saying, "Yes, this is indeed what you have been needing and searching for. You have been needing to know me as Love—not only as Redeemer and Savior, but by my real name of Love. And if from now on you are to be united with me, then you too must walk in the fire of my love and become a flaming torch of love yourself."

Such passages as these became veritable rays of illumination to my soul: "To die to self and be delivered from its power, cannot be done by active resistance ... The one immediate unerring way, is the way of patience, meekness, humility and utter resignation and surrender to God ... We must believe that by turning and giving ourselves to these virtues is as certain and immediate a way of being possessed and blessed by their power as when sinners turn to Christ to be helped and saved by him ... For when I exhort you to turn in faith to the Lamb of God, and ask you what the Lamb of God means, must you not tell me that he was, and is, the perfection and patience and humility and resignation to God expressed in Jesus Christ?

"Therefore is not a hunger and thirst for these things the very same as a hunger and thirst for him? Consequently every sincere wish and desire which presses after these virtues and longs to be governed by them, is an immediate, direct application to Christ, is worshiping and falling down before him, is giving up your self to him and the very perfection of faith in him . . .

"Love is the Christ of God. Nothing is uneasy, unsatisfied or restless but because it is not governed by love or attained the full birth of the Spirit of Love. Divine love is a new life and a new nature, and introduces you into a new world . . When divine love is born in the soul, all childish images of good and evil are done away. If the Spirit of Love is really born in you . . . you know it by the price you have paid for it in the many deaths to self which you have suffered before the Spirit of Love came to birth in you."

Another shining flash of illumination came to me through the emphasis which William Law places on the necessity for universal love.

The flame of true love derived from God can never remain love for one particular person only, or for a particular circle of loved ones, but it must become universal, namely love for all mankind. He writes: "The greatest idea that we can frame of God is when we conceive him to be a being of infinite love and goodness, using an infinite wisdom and power for the common good and happiness of all his creatures. The highest notion therefore that we can conceive of man, is to conceive of him as like God in this respect as he can be. There is nothing more acceptable to God than an universal, fervent love to all mankind, wishing and praying for their happiness as much as for our own.

"We must practice in our hearts the love of all, because it is not Christian love until it is the love of all. Acts of love which proceed not from a principle of universal love, are but like acts of justice that proceed from a heart not disposed to universal justice but only to a favored few. A love which is not universal, may indeed have tenderness and affection, but it has nothing of righteousness in it . . . it is such a love as publicans and heathens practice." Love is not any natural tenderness which is more or less in people according to their constitutions. But a love which loves all things in God. It is a holy fire which cleanses and purifies.

"If I hate or despise any one man in the world, I hate something which God cannot hate, and despise that which he loves . . . No one is of the spirit of Christ unless he has the utmost compassion for sinners. Nor is there any greater sign of your own perfection than when you find yourself all love and compassion towards them that are very weak and defective. And on the other hand you have never less reason to be pleased with yourself than when you find yourself most angry and offended at the behavior of others. All sin is certainly to be hated and abhorred, but we must set ourselves against sin as we do against sickness and disease, by showing ourselves tender and compassionate to the sick and the diseased.

"How then is it possible to love a good and a bad man to the same degree? Just as it is possible to be just and faithful to a good man as well as to an evil man. You are in no difficulty about performing justice to a bad man ... because justice and faithfulness are founded upon reasons which never vary and which do not depend upon the merits of men. And love is founded upon the same unchanging reasons."

It will surely repay everyone of us to read and re-read and ponder and meditate upon such passages as these from *The Spirit of Love* and *The Serious Call*.

"William Law is one of the most powerful and suggestive writers on the Christian life ... his readers will rise up from these books saying, these are the two best books in the world ... in their way, and on such subjects show me another two books like them in the world." So wrote Andrew Murray and Christopher Walton. And Dr. Alexander Whyte said the same thing over and over again in other words. And what a multitude of other grateful souls have looked up to their Lord and echoed the same gratitude.

The more I read these books and was led into the experience of which they write, the more convinced I became that this is the true baptism with the Holy Spirit which is promised to the true followers of the Lord Jesus Christ. "He shall baptize you with the Holy Ghost and with fire." The Spirit of Burning, the Spirit of Holy Love.

Holiness is a most lovely word in the Bible sense. It means to be separated and set apart; separated, in fact, from all that is not love and set apart for one purpose only, that the Spirit of Holy Love may dwell in us and think in us and express himself through us. Holy people are people in whom holy love is incarnate.

Righteousness, or rightness, is everything which is in harmony with love, just as unrighteousness or unrightness, is everything out of harmony with holy love. Everything therefore which breaks the royal law of love is evil. There is no evil except in the negation of love, which is the law on which God has founded his whole universe. Sin is love turned inward to the self, instead of outward to God our Creator and to all mankind whom he has created.

"Our God is a consuming fire," says the Old Testament, and the New Testament repeats and perfectly explains this statement by saying, "God is love." God is holy love, a fire of love which consumes and destroys all that is antagonistic to the nature of holy love, and which purifies and liberates into a new kind of life all who receive the nature of the fire into themselves.

This God who is a consuming fire of holy

love, has founded the whole universe on this same royal law of love, and to obey it is to fulfill the law of our own being. If we cease to love we act contrary to the law of our nature and we break the harmony of our personality. When this one law on which God had founded his universe is broken, everything breaks down and falls into confusion and chaos. It is as though a wrench has been thrown into the works, or as if grit and sand have got into the gas tank of a car and thus make it impossible for the car to fulfill the purpose for which it was made. It simply will not go.

We discover that this royal law is written in every part of our three-fold nature—spirit, soul and body. Even the tissues and cells and nerves and glands of our body respond to the law of love. When we are loving our neighbors as ourselves we tend to be well and happy. As soon as we break it, disintegration of the whole personality begins. To harbor thoughts (and the feelings which are created by such thoughts) of hatred, resentment, bitterness, jealousy, envy, rage, spite, pride and contempt of others, is to poison ourselves in body as well as mind and spirit.

Love, then, is the one unmistakable sign of "baptism with the Holy Spirit." "He shall baptize you with the Holy Ghost and with fire." The results of such a baptism by the Holy Spirit of Love reveal themselves in a continual turning outward from ourselves of all the love energy which hitherto has been lavished upon the self. Any other experience which claims to be a baptism with the Holy Spirit, on the sole ground that it is accompanied by the phenomena of speaking with tongues or even power to heal, unless it results in a life of continual universal love, must be a spurious claim. The apostle Paul emphasizes this with the utmost clearness in the thirteenth chapter of first Corinthians:

"Though I speak with the tongues of men and angels, and have not love, I am become as sounding brass and as a tinkling cymbal. And though I have the gift of prophecy and understand all mysteries and all knowledge, and though I have all faith so that I could remove mountains, and have not love, I am nothing."

The sign of true love, we remember, is that it is universal love, love to all, without exception, not just to a chosen few or to a special coterie of particular Christians.

And now we have to ask the great question,

What is love?

CHAPTER 10
Love in Oneness

"Father, I pray . . . that they all may be one: as thou, Father, art in me and I in thee, that they also may be one in us . . . I in them and thou in me that they may be made perfect in one . . . and that the world may know that . . . thou hast loved them as thou hast loved me" (John 17:21-23).

There was one question which had often perplexed my mind. If God is love and if God was incarnate in the Lord Jesus Christ, why is he not called Love in the New Testament. For it is clear that Love is a Person, the Lord Jesus Christ himself, and yet we are not told in so many words that he was incarnate Love.

Surely the answer is that love is a word so easily misunderstood and debased and distorted that we could never grasp its true meaning from the word itself. We have seen too many caricatures called love, and too many false expressions of it. So that the word love has become like debased coin. It conveys a wrong meaning to our understanding, and is always too inadequate to express the real thing. Therefore it has been perfectly expressed for us in a Person.

When we look at the Lord Jesus as he is revealed to us in the Gospels, we have a true and perfect portrait of Love himself and a trustworthy standard and pattern by which to judge everything which calls itself love. Perfect Love has been manifested to the world, and the name he bears is Jesus (Savior) because his Saviorhood is the most perfect expression of love—of himself.

How, then, does Love manifest himself? and what is the nature of his love, that we may see whether it is true love which dwells in our hearts also?

There is one unique characteristic and quality in true love, which is the hallmark and guarantee of the real thing. Love is a passionate desire for oneness. The Lord Jesus himself gives us this definition of love: "I pray . . . that they all may be one, as thou, Father, art in me and I in thee, that they also may be one in us . . . that they may be one even as we are one. I in them and thou in me, that they may be made perfect in one . . and that the world may know that thou hast sent me, and that thou hast loved them as thou hast loved me" (John 17: 21-23).

The final test of true love is this desire for oneness. We see this characteristic exhibited in beautiful clarity in the symbols of human love and marriage union, the passion of two people to become one with each other. But this is human love and is only a faint picture of the nature of divine love.

Human love lifted on to a higher plane altogether becomes a passion to become one with God and with all the creatures he has made. On the human plane there must of course be some who quite rightly mean more to us than others, and with whom we achieve greater oneness. But we are so created by the God of Love, from whom we derive our very being, that nothing can perfectly satisfy us until we are enabled to turn all the love energy outward in universal love to God and to all men.

God so loved the world of men, that he became man in order that he might be made one with them. God has united himself with the human race, even in their fallen condition. This began to be brought home to my heart and understanding through an unforgettable experience a few years ago.

It so happened that throughout the whole Easter weekend that year, I was flying half-way around the world, from Israel to New Zealand. Sitting for three days in the plane, alternately reading the Easter story and meditating upon it, and looking out of the window down on the crowded countries over which we were flying, it came to me with a vividness and power which I had never before known, that I was looking down on the world of men which God loved so much that he must become one with it in a marriage union which cannot be broken or ended.

That union he consummated in the incarnation and upon the cross when he revealed his complete identification with us, even in our sins and misery. To such extremities this passion for oneness with the beloved object carried the eternal God of Love. And it is from that burning, flaming fire of holy love that our own hearts are to be kindled with a like passion.

Thus we see quite clearly that to love is to recognize our oneness with all whom God has created, and to have a passionate desire to realize this oneness fully. William Law points out that "love is not Christian love until it is universal, until it includes all and not just some."

Of course, as soon as we begin to understand this tremendous truth we are overwhelmed by the impossibility of coming up to the standard. We talk about the widespread lack of conviction of sin in our generation. So many people declare emphatically that they are not sinners. Even we who are Christians often feel terribly self-righteous and smug in our inmost thoughts, especially when we compare ourselves with others. But the moment we realize that sin is any, and every, breaking of this law of universal love, and a refusal to acknowledge our oneness with others, or even to desire that oneness, then the overwhelming conviction of being helpless and hopeless sinners does break upon us.

We all know perfectly well that naturally we do not love even our nearest and dearest as ourselves; and that there are heaps and heaps of people that we do not desire to love or to be one with, indeed, the further we can emphasize the distance between us, the better! There are people that we dislike intensely, whom we always avoid if possible, with whom we are temperamentally incompatible, people we label as odd, exasperating, incredibly stupid, obstinate, self-opinionated, dogmatic, appallingly selfish, or altogether impossible.

Does it not seem likely, therefore, that the reason why there is so little conviction of sin in the world today is because multitudes of non-Christian people see so little in professing Christians to convict them? How often do they see a company of men and women obviously aflame with love and with a passion for oneness? If every Christian was like a burning bush on fire with love, loving one another as themselves, in spite of diversity of temperament, gifts, character, creed and doctrine, would not people be convicted at once?

"See how these Christians love each other!" cried the pagans of old, and flocked to listen to these transformed men and women who had been fused together in one by the welding flame of love.

Why do so many of us fail to realize this? How can we be so blind? When it does break upon us our hearts instantly cry out despairingly: "But I can't love! I can't obey the royal law! There are some people I simply cannot love!"

Until we discover the secret of universal love we can never fulfill the purpose of our creation.

First, let us face up to the one great fact. We are one. We have been created one whether we like it or not. Only when we acknowledge this truth, and pray the Savior to help us realize our oneness, can it become possible to obey the law of love.

For human nature is such that we are one in needing to be loved if we are to become what our Creator means us to be and to achieve perfect development.

We are surrounded by multitudes of individuals who, without exception, cry out in the depths of their hearts, "I need to be loved. I can't become what I am meant to be, and I cannot know the fulfillment, unless I am loved."

The emotional people who openly express this universal craving for love, instead of carefully covering it over with decent reserve, who cry out, "Oh, I do want to be loved! I must have love!" are called sentimental and are despised as weak and unbalanced creatures because they make no pretense at hiding this basic need of human nature. The craving is undoubtedly implanted in all of us without exception, and the fact is that we cannot become what we long to be, and are meant to be, unless we are loved.

The poverty and misery of those who are despised by their fellows, ostracized and left lonely and unwanted, is truly frightful. The poor, the beggars, the outcasts whom nobody loves, how can they possibly become what they were created to be, radiant sons and daughters of God? It is the worst torment that the world can provide to feel unwanted by everyone. Let one person, however, come along who feels and expresses their love and desire for friendship and for oneness, then that stunted, starved and withering life is transformed. It bursts into blossom and will be able to thrive in the midst of the most depressing and frustrating circumstances possible. A sense of being loved can work miracles in the most unpromising personality.

But more than this, we are also one in our

need to love others (to love all others), if we are to know true fulfillment and be made perfectly conformable to the perfect pattern our Creator has designed for us.

"I can love those who love me, but I can't love those who don't love me or who obviously dislike or hate me."

That is the normal reaction of all of us who have lost the power to obey the royal law of love. A great many Christians, if they are honest with themselves, know that this is the exact level on which they live, even though they claim to be followers of Jesus Christ who is the Lord of love. "I can love those that love me, but not those who don't, and why should I try to?" we exclaim to ourselves, and then, with a shock, hear our Lord saying:

"If ye love them which love you, what reward have you? Do not even the publicans the same? But I say unto you, Love your enemies, bless them that curse you, do good to them that hate you and pray for them that despitefully use you and persecute you. That ye may be the children of your Father which is in heaven, for he maketh his sun to rise on the evil and on the good and sendeth rain on the just and on the unjust. Be ye therefore perfect as your Father which is in heaven is perfect" (Matt. 5:44, 45, 48).

Yes, we must realize that we cannot be perfect until we are made perfect in love. We are not being saved and delivered from sin; our Lord has died in vain, as far as we are concerned, unless we have begun to allow him to turn our love-energy outward from self, upward to himself, and around on all others with whom we are in contact. This is the one law of our being. We must be loved and we must love, for love creates and awakens love.

Love is wonderfully creative. God is love, and God is the Creator of all, and love is the only really creative power in the universe.

Here is a common, everyday illustration of the creativity of love, to illustrate why we need it, and the harm and the damage we do to each other when we withhold it. Have you not noticed that if you meet someone who dislikes you, and they refuse to smile at you and even scowl or cross the street or look the other way, how quickly there awakens and stirs in you a feeling of resentment or pain or answering dislike? That person has created in you the same feelings which are in their own heart.

If you have to work in the presence of someone who actively dislikes or despises you, even though they may not often express it in words, how it paralyzes and cripples you and brings out all the worst that is in you. Have you ever found yourself really helped by someone you know dislikes you? Or able to respond quickly to a Christian who has felt led to speak to you on some matter, for your own good, when you know and feel that one disapproves of you, or despises you, and is only speaking because their feelings are so jarred by you that they are determined they must change you? No, you cannot be helped by that person. Indeed, they rather hinder than help you.

In the same way, however, if you meet someone in the street or the train who smiles at you and greets you as though they were really glad to see you, or expresses some gracious and kindly interest in you, how instantly creative such an attitude is. Joy awakens in you, you feel stirred on to greater efforts, and something comes to life in you that you were not conscious of before. Are not the friends who help you, the ones who love you in spite of your faults, and who do not allow those faults to make any difference in their love to you, so that they do not get exasperated and infuriated with you? These are the disciples who share the creative power of their Lord.

Of course it is so. Love is creative, and dislike and lack of love are destructive and we feel this (almost unconsciously) the whole time. Thus, when we refuse to love, and when we ignore and disdain others, it is not just a negative attitude. We are doing them actual harm, for unless they are garrisoned by love themselves and know the secret of the Lord and are actively loving us as he has taught them to, there will awaken in them active dislike and ill will.

Then arises another great question. How can we love the unlovely and the sin-marred, the altogether unattractive, even the criminal and the vicious? How can we possibly desire to feel one with them? Indeed, ought we even to desire to do so? Surely love cannot love the unlovely and those who are antagonistic to love?

The answer, of course, is to be found in the Lord Jesus, incarnate Love himself. How did he solve this problem? How did he react to the unlovely and to the enemies of love?

By becoming incarnate in fallen mankind; making himself the actual representative of the hideous, sin-blemished and sin-deformed human race. "God commendeth his love towards us in that, while we were yet sinners, Christ died for us." Christ insisted, as man, in realizing his oneness with us all while we were yet sinners.

Then can the Lord of love really love the unlovely? Alter the question by one word and let each of us ask ourselves, "Can the Lord of love really love me? For I am so unlovely and sin-defiled." What can he possibly see to like, much less to love, in you and me, confirmed breakers as we are, of his perfect and royal law of love?

Can he love us, we who are so selfish, ugly and blemished, with so many unlovely habits? Yes, we know he does. How does he love us? When we understand that we shall be able to understand how he can help us to love the unlovely and to realize our oneness with even the most unattractive.

The answer is that he looks upon us with an infinite compassion. He sees us as a race of people hideously disfigured and deformed by a loathsome disease; he sees the whole body of mankind corrupted and sick and dying. "The whole head is sick and the whole heart faint. From the sole of the foot even unto the head there is no soundness in it, but wounds and bruises and putrifying sores: they have not been closed, neither bound up, neither mollified with ointment" (Isa. 1:5-6).

He knows, too, that we cannot help ourselves, for we were born into this corrupted and diseased human race. In some people the horrible symptoms of sin are appallingly evident; in others, who are still young and outwardly lovely, there may be apparent only a few little blemishes, but these reveal to the great Physician the presence of the same awful disease. He sees us as sick unto death, and has compassion upon us, for he said:

"They that are whole need not a physician but they that are sick." "The Son of Man is come to seek and to save that which is lost."

Surely, we who are followers of the Lord of love and members of his Body, do need a revolution in our understanding of sin and in our attitude to these multitudes of men and women and little children who, like ourselves, have all been born with an incurable disease, greatly sinned against as well as sinning against others, and who are utterly unable to cure themselves.

"Would you," says Doctor Alexander

Whyte, "hate or strike back at a blind man who stumbled against you in the street? Or retaliate at a maniac on his way to the mad-house? And shall we retaliate on a miserable man driven mad with diabolical passion or diseased with ill will?"

All visible sins in men and women are symptoms manifesting this deadly disease, and they should awaken in us infinite compassion as well as horror.

The great Physician "is able to have compassion on them that are out of the way" (Heb. 5:2). "Seeing the multitudes he was moved with compassion on them" (Matt. 9:36). "For God sent not his Son into the world to condemn the world; but that the world, through him, might be saved" (John 3:17).

Nowhere in he gospel does our Lord and Savior condemn sinners, though he warns continually. His denunciations and condemnations were all spoken to those who saw and beheld him—the great Physician and his power to heal the sin-sick and to save the fallen, and who refused to be healed themselves. It was to professedly religious people that he spoke of condemnation, to those who had light and rejected it; and to those who refused to confess that they were among the sin-sick and who rejected the cure which he offered them at such incredible cost to himself. "This," said he, "is the condemnation, that light is come into the world, and men love darkness rather than light" (John 3:19).

143

This is the condemnation, the only condemnation that he uttered, and he spoke it to the religious leaders of Israel before whose very eyes he was manifested as the light of the world.

If we, too, desire to realize our oneness with sinners and to love them creatively as Christ loved us, then our whole thought attitude towards them may need to be changed. The eyes of our understanding must be opened so that we shall be able to see them (even the unloveliest of them) in their hopeless need and misery as sin-sick and diseased unto death. Then all that is foul and ugly and unclean (or merely unattractive) will awaken in us a passionate desire to share, if possible, in bringing about their healing and transformation through the saving power of Christ.

CHAPTER 11
True Ground of Unity

"He that hath my commandments and keepeth them, he it is that loveth me, and he that loveth me shall be loved of my Father, and I will love him, and will manifest myself to him ... and we will come unto him and make our abode with him" (John 14:21-23).

"Everyone that loveth is born of God and knoweth God" (1 John 4:7).

There is another aspect of this greatest of all subjects—the oneness of love. This must surely weigh upon our hearts in the most overwhelming way, namely the terrible and tragic situation presented to the non-Christian world of the Church of Christ as a great company of people in all lands, who to all intents and purposes do not seem to be one in more than the name of Christian, and who, moreover, often evince no desire at all for this oneness with each other which was the passionate desire of their Lord for them, and which was to be their greatest witness to the world.

I remember so well, years ago, on the mission field, listening to two missionary friends who seemed to view this problem from two different angles. One of them said:

"If anyone teaches erroneous doctrine contrary to the word of God, I will not have fellowship with that person. It would be disloyalty to my Lord if I did not separate myself from them completely."

Whereas the second one said: "If anyone really loves the Lord Jesus Christ sincerely, and honestly desires to obey him according to the light which he has received, I must have fellowship with that person, no matter how erroneous some of his beliefs seem to be. Though I heartily disagree with those beliefs and feel bound to say so, I cannot separate from my fellow lover of the Lord as though he were not a member of the Body and had no life in him."

It cannot be denied that the problem is a very great one, for how, we ask, can there be oneness and unity when there are countless multitudes of Christian people disagreeing on many points of doctrine and belief, and considering one another's beliefs and practices as error, superstition, heresy and dangerous perversions of the truth, while at the same time all the different groups claim the authority of Christ and his apostles in support of their own views? Surely it is impossible to feel an honest and sincere oneness with those with whom we disagree?

If the basis of our unity is purity of doctrine and practice, then it is impossible.

But the basis of our unity is a Person, the Lord Jesus Christ, who was God incarnate in the flesh. It is not our understanding of his teaching and belief in his atoning death which unites us (for our apprehension of truth is so diverse), but our longing to worship and obey him according to the light which we have. He is the ground of our oneness.

Diversity of belief and understanding need never mean disunity—it will call for still more love. We are not to accept one another's dogmas and interpretations and say they are all right, but to remind ourselves that we are all tainted with error and distortion and that the only way to see more truth is to love more. In actual fact, to repudiate any member of the body will mean some degree of blindness; but to love more will mean the entrance of more light. It is love which enables God to reveal himself to us individually and collectively. And love enables us to help others to a fuller understanding of truth.

"Lord, how wilt thou manifest thyself unto us and not unto the world?" Jesus answered, "If a man love me . . . we will come unto him and make our abode with him . . . He that loveth me shall be loved of my Father and I will love him and will manifest myself unto him" (John 14:21-23).

If a man love me, he shall see!

This is the great principle for knowing God and for understanding the truth, "love me."

If only we would accept the fact that we all are wrong in some respects, and that lack of love and oneness lies at the bottom of our varying interpretations of the truth, surely we would be willing to go back to our first love and acknowledge our oneness.

"In this oneness standeth the life of all mankind!" exclaimed Mother Julian of Norwich, and surely love had led her right back to the starting place for understanding truth.

It does seem that far and away the most diabolical and subtle victory achieved by the enemy of souls, is the successful way in which he has persuaded the Christian church as a whole, and multitudes of individual Christians, to repudiate their oneness and to substitute a false principle of unity. He has persuaded them that it is right for them to use his own deadliest weapon (invented in hell)—the weapon of complete separation from all with whom we do not agree. As a matter of dreadful fact, the devil actually taught the professing Church of Christ at a very early stage in her history, the secret of splitting the atom of unity, and there has been constant and horrifying disintegration ever since.

Before the canon of Holy Scripture was closed, the risen Lord clearly warned his Church against using this deadly atom bomb of the devil's devising and drew attention to the danger of doing so in the most solemn way. In his message to the church of Ephesus, the first of the seven messages which he sent through his servant John, he said warningly:

"I have somewhat against thee. Thou hast left thy first love. Remember, therefore, from whence thou art fallen and repent and do the first works (of love), or else I will come unto thee quickly and will remove thy candlestick out of its place, unless thou repent" (Rev. 2:4, 5).

It is quite evident that already the enemy had been trying to split the Church by deceiving her with a false method for preserving Christian unity, namely separation instead of love. When she began to follow the false principle she began to destroy her witness to the world and embarked upon a long and tragic history of repeated separations. The atom of love and unity was split.

As nowhere is it permitted in the Scriptures for a Christian wife and husband to separate because they disagree, so nowhere is it permitted to members of the body of

Christ to repudiate one another and to separate from each other on the ground of disagreement, either in interpretation of the Scriptures, church practice or church claims, however erroneous they may be. Our only separation is to be from everything out of harmony with love and from unloving practices towards others, from all sin and self love.

Certainly the Scriptures do authorize us to express our complete disagreement with what we believe to be unsound doctrine, and even more strongly with unsound practices which are a contradiction of love.

"Preach the word, be instant in season, out of season; reprove, rebuke, exhort with all long-suffering and doctrine" (2 Tim. 4:2).

"Whose mouths must be stopped, teaching things which they ought not. Rebuke them sharply." But not a word about repudiating them as members of the body of Christ.

One verse is always quoted in favor of separation, i.e., 2 John 10: "If there come any unto you and have not this doctrine, receive him not into your house, neither bid him God-speed." We see that this doctrine is the doctrine (or teaching) of Jesus Christ and in verse 7 the warning is clearly against those deceivers who confess not that Christ (Messiah) has come in the flesh; namely those who deny that Jesus was the Christ, just as the Jews do until this day, and who contradict his teaching.

Obviously such teachers were not even

Christians, and therefore were not to be received and entertained as though they were Christian messengers and brethren. And in all passages where such strong terms are used it will be found that they are applied to people who do not acknowledge the Lord Jesus Christ and contradict his clear teaching. Differences of interpretation about his teaching and meaning are no cause for separation, but rejection of his claims is.

How tragically and overwhelmingly successful the devil has been in deluding so many into the belief that Christian separation authorizes the repudiation and excommunication of those who differ in interpretation and belief. This, indeed, has been his deadliest weapon.

During century after century different sections of the Church have made use of his diabolical atom bomb and have persecuted and excommunicated the saints of God. In our own day and generation we are no longer allowed to go to the extreme of imprisoning and burning one another, though we still continue to repudiate, denounce and condemn one another and even (and that amongst the sincerest Christians) refuse to allow fellow members of the body of Christ to share in the communion service of love and fellowship.

Indeed, the more earnest and zealous for the truth a particular sect or group may be, the more fanatical, in some cases, is their repudiation of everyone else, even to the extreme of denouncing their fellow Christians as deluded by the devil.

That there are devil-inspired delusions among Christians is, alas, not to be denied, and terribly destructive and dangerous they are. Can there in actual fact, however, be any devil-inspired delusion more terrible and destructive than this one with which he has succeeded in innoculating practically every section of the Christian Church, namely that when Christ prayed for his people that they might be one, he meant that they were to repudiate one another and to separate from all those with whom they disagree?

A favorite illustration often used to bolster up this principle of separation is that of a number of apples lying together on a shelf, some of which are in a state of decay. It is pointed out quite undeniably, that if the good apples are left in contact with the bad ones, they will not make the bad ones good, but will themselves become infected by the decay and become corrupted by the bad ones with which they remain in contact.

What is not so often pointed out is that even the separated apples, if left a little longer, will begin to decay in their own isolated group, and that both the already decaying apples and those which yet show no signs of going bad, can only remain untainted and truly alive and growing and developing as long as they remain together on the tree which nourishes them with its life.

Many utterly devoted and sincere Christians have felt themselves called to complete separation from corrupted churches so that they may be able to manifest to the world "a true church" such as Christ first founded, but over and over again it seems that God has allowed them to demonstrate the truth that unity cannot be achieved by separation but only by love which is oneness. Though these separated groups are often used and blessed by God in many ways and have proved a great challenge to the dead companies which they left, they have never found unity but only the beginning of sad internal disintegration and further separating.

Love is the welding flame by which the true Church of Christ is welded together. It is love which opens our blind eyes and enables us to see truth and to follow on to know the Lord. Love is the answer to the whole problem of a divided Church. John, the beloved disciple, told us so right at the very beginning:

"Beloved, let us love one another: for love is of God: and everyone that loveth is born of God and knoweth God ... If we love one another, God dwelleth in us and his love is perfected in us" (1 John 4:7, 12).

CHAPTER 12

Revelation Made by Jesus Christ

"I have manifested thy name unto the men which thou gavest me out of the world . . . I have given unto them the words which thou gavest me, and they have received them and have known surely that I came out from thee, and they have believed that thou didst send me . . . I have declared unto them thy name and will declare it, that the love wherewith thou hast loved me may be in them and I in them" (John 17:6, 8, 26).

How strangely and beautifully God illumines our understanding and gradually develops our capacity to see and understand more, so that the Scriptures seem constantly to unfold to us new and richer conceptions of the truth as we are able to bear it. Perhaps most of all is this the case with our understanding of the great central truths of the Christian faith, those lovely and dazzling mysteries which the more we meditate and ponder upon them, the more almost blindingly aglow with light they become.

The height and the depth and the length and the breadth of the mysteries of love we never shall understand with these finite minds of ours. But every new glimpse that we do get, and every new ray of light which breaks into our minds and hearts, seems to work a revolution in our ideas, in our love and in our power to witness to others.

Before I bring this book to a close, I would like to try to share (if it can be at all possible to do so through the medium of words) one of the most transforming conceptions about the revelation of God given to us by the incarnation and death and resurrection of our Lord and Savior Jesus Christ which has begun shining in my mind with a glory and radiance beyond anything understood before. It must have been germinating like a seed in my mind for well over twenty years, gradually developing, and then all of a sudden, unfolding in unspeakable beauty and glory and yet overwhelming awe.

As a young Christian my first conception of God represented him to me as a holy God, high and lifted up and inhabiting eternity; seated on the throne of the universe and of purer eyes than to see evil. He was entirely unapproachable by sinners, save through a mediator, his son Jesus Christ. I knew that the Scriptures also said, "His eyes run to and fro throughout the whole earth" and that he knows everything and nothing can be hidden from him, that even the hairs of our head are numbered and so is every blade of grass and every speck of dust that blows about in the universe.

But I conceived of him as cognizant of it all in an absolutely impersonal way (except of those who were brought into a personal relationship with him through Jesus Christ). He was, I vaguely supposed, entirely above and beyond the reach of suffering, the one, eternal spirit who was to be worshipped and adored. But he was also to be loved, because, wonder of wonders, and mystery of mysteries, once, two thousand years ago, he chose to become incarnate and to visit this world in great humility in Jesus Christ our Savior.

Thus for thirty-three years he did actually experience our human nature and become acquainted with grief, and for six awful hours on the cross did endure appalling human agony and did actually die a terrible physical death. And so now he does know through personal experience what it feels like; just as a doctor can understand and feel for a patient who must undergo a painful operation which the doctor himself has also undergone, even though he no longer feels the pain in the way the patient feels it.

I was quite sure that when Christ arose again from the dead and returned to the glory of the Father which was his before the world began, all his sufferings were over and he now waited for sinful men and women to accept what he had done for them during those thirty-three years of human life and the six awful hours upon the cross. (I pushed aside the thought which did sometimes intrude, that his atoning sufferings lasted a much shorter time than the agonies which he allows multitudes of his followers to suffer, sometimes even for years, not to mention the long drawn-out torments of countless millions dying of lingering disease or languishing in prison for life.)

But I was absolutely certain that now he is past the reach of all suffering, in a condition and state where suffering and sorrow cannot be felt.

Though it is more than twenty years ago now, I never can forget the shock of horror and repudiation of the very idea with which I reacted to a passage in a book in which a minister shared some new thoughts which had been coming to him in connection with the sufferings which God must still undergo just because he is cognizant of everything which goes on in this sin-ruined world.

If we could know, he wrote, about all the suffering and sorrow and sin in one tiny hamlet, we would break down, but God knows and is cognizant of all the sin and the horror of its manifestations and results all over the world. Not a single detail is unknown to him. And then the writer of the book described his own reactions while visiting in the slums of a great city, when it was necessary for him to go to some foul den of thieves, or some haunt of evil, on an errand of love and mercy. He wrote, "I pity, I sympathize, I try to help, and then I come home. And then I bathe myself and I eat and I sleep and I am away from it all. But he stays there. He is still in that foul den, that slum, that brothel. He remains cognizant of it all."

That was the very first time that such an idea had ever been suggested to my mind, and it appalled me. With my whole will I longed to reject it—the mere thought was too awful: a suffering God instead of the high and lofty one, who had only needed to suffer once in order to atone for all the world's sorrow and anguish and sin. But there it was and I could not escape the awful truth that God, being omnipresent, so far from being apart from the world's suffering and anguish must be conscious of it all the time and, moreover, conscious of the whole sum total of it all the time and never able to escape from it. And feeling it all with the anguish of holy love.

It was an appalling thought. The God

whom I had supposed (because I misunderstood the term) to be of purer eyes than to see evil much less to feel its effects in any way, except a feeling of great compassion that sinners should have brought upon themselves so much suffering and shame, now had to be conceived of as absolutely conscious of all the sin and evil everywhere and to suffer as a result. A suffering God! Ah! how can I possible describe the overwhelming revolution in my whole thought about God which such a new and overwhelming conception brought about? The sin of the world was still hurting him. He was not above and beyond it all. But still, revolutionary as this new idea was, I still thought of him as suffering, as it were, from without, looking on at our agony and sin and the torments we endure, and suffering in much the same way as a loving and heart-broken father or mother suffers while tending a child in some agonizing illness, or as a husband suffers while nursing a wife dying with cancer. Suffering is the anguished sympathy of love.

It took another twenty years for that seed thought to germinate and develop in my mind until it unfolded and opened out in my understanding in a still more overwhelming realization. I was reading Ernest Raymond's book on St. Francis of Assisi, and came to the description of Francis, just after his conversion, riding on horseback near the crossroads where stood a leper hospital. He had such a horror of lepers and of the stench coming forth from the Lazar house that generally he avoided the place altogether. But on this occasion, lost in thought, he did not notice where he was until suddenly his horse shied, and then he saw a leper standing in the path before him, asking for alms.

His first impulse was to fling his purse to the poor wretch and then spur his horse away from the spot as quickly as possible. "But was not the leper with his eaten face and his outcast's uniform a symbol of suffering and poverty? Before he could think again, leaping from his horse and forcing himself all the time, he went to the leper, put all his money in his hand and then lifted that hand and kissed it. And in Italy the kiss of the hand is the kiss of reverence to the representative of Christ."

I have quoted the exact words which had a totally unexpected and overwhelming effect upon me. For once again, just as twenty years before, some veil seemed suddenly torn away from my understanding, and in another blinding flash of insight I beheld another and still more appalling truth. It was almost as though I saw a new God altogether; and yet I knew that all the time the truth had been revealed and I ought to have seen it long ago.

Francis suddenly saw (and at that moment I saw with him) what our Lord Jesus has revealed about God through his choosing to become incarnate in a man—namely that he is conscious of himself in all men, conscious of himself present in a man with an eaten face, living amid a never-ceasing stench, despised and feared by everyone, an outcast from all his fellowmen save those who were lepers also. God knowing and feeling exactly what it was like because he has deliberately chosen to extend his own consciousness into us all. Indeed, we could not exist at all unless he did so.

Until that moment I had thought of God as conscious of everything from without, as a loving Father looking on in agony at our terrible condition. But now I saw, and was blinded by the sight, that he is conscious of it from within.

From that moment the revelation which he made of himself when he became incarnate as a man, took on an absolutely new meaning and significance. Once, in the fullness of time, when we were able to be shown, God in Jesus Christ revealed himself to us and the truth about himself. As this broke upon me, all that had seemed so mysterious and difficult to account for suddenly became crystal clear with the clarity of things revealed by a flash of lightning, though the details, of course, had to be assimilated and meditated on with awe and adoring worship, and absorbed little by little.

God actually insisting on becoming in some way incarnate in the whole human race, in every human creature whom he has made, by extending his consciousness into them so that he knows exactly how they feel and how they react, and how they suffer the awful and tormenting consequences of their own wrong choices and self-love and sin. Not apart from us as an onlooker, but within, as a sharer in it, identified with us while we are yet sinners.

This is what the saints mean when they speak of God as immanent. Immanence—not pantheism. Pantheists say that as God is in everything the sum total of everything must be God. But surely immanence means that the Creator who has conceived everything and brought it into existence, has extended into all human creatures whom he has made, his own consciousness. Not interfering with free will, but feeling and conscious of everything which we feel, and conscious of himself seeking to help us and to bring us back to our lost consciousness of himself. God conscious of what it means for us to be fallen sin-diseased souls. God extending his consciousness into mankind, into the whole fallen human race.

Is not this sending forth of his own consciousness of himself the "proceeding forth from the Father of the Son of God" to become also Son of Man? Is not this suffering consciousness of God, the Lamb of God who beareth the sin of the world? "Jesus said . . . I proceeded forth and came from God, neither came I of myself, but he sent me" (John 8:42). What a wonderful new ray of illumination on the mystery of the Trinity this new conception of the truth has brought to my own mind. All the Scriptures indeed seem to have come alive in an absolutely new way.

As soon as this realization broke upon me I understood that we, we fallen sin-diseased mankind, are God's cross. This surely was the next overwhelming part of the revelation which our Lord Jesus made. God's consciousness extended into sinners who reject him and put him on a cross, seeking to get rid of him. Their sins, as it were, his crucifixion.

Our Lord had to make this dreadful revelation in all its fullness, and surely that is why, when he hung on the cross and they mocked him and cried, "Save thyself and come down from the cross" he made no response, only wrought out the awful revelation of the awful truth. He could not come down from his cross if he were to give us a true revelation, for the truth is that our Creator and God will not come down from his cross, will not save himself and withdraw his consciousness from us until we take him down by responding to him and allowing him to save us from our sin, so that he may be conscious of his life at last entering into us and raising us up to newness of life.

I read somewhere that there is a picture in one of the art galleries in Europe which depicts the expulsion of Adam and Eve from the Garden of Eden. In the picture Eden lies behind them and an angel with a flaming sword guards the gate. Before them stretches a waste of briars and thorns. But Adam and Eve are not pictured as looking back with a sorrowful longing to Eden, nor are they looking with shrinking fear at the wilderness before them. The artist has depicted them as looking up towards heaven, awe-struck and overwhelmed with horror, where a great cross appears in the sky and the one they had known and worshipped in the Garden of Eden, as he walked with them in the cool of the evening, is now nailed upon the cross.

Is not the truth, the overwhelming truth, this fact, that not just once only, for six hours when Jesus the Incarnate Word hung upon the cross and died a physical death, did God bear the sin of the world, but from the first moment of man's sinning, his cross began. Once, when the fullness of time was come and men at last could be shown the truth, for six hours the veil was drawn aside, as it were, and Christ made visible what is happening all the time, and has been happening from the moment of man's fall.

This will continue to happen as long as mankind continues to sin, namely God himself bearing it all and agonizing with us, but still more for us, in our sin. This world of men is his cross. You and I have been his cross and still are unless he had been able to come down from his cross in us and to be conscious in us of resurrection life. When he created man, he purposed that it should be so; that he would extend his own consciousness into us, and not even the fall changed his purpose. No, he would go through with it, bearing and feeling all that our sin and self-will should bring into existence, suffering it all with us.

He has extended his consciousness into every human being he has created (though man's consciousness of God died with the first sin), into every suffering babe and child, every debased criminal, every sadist, every tormented drug addict, every fallen prostitute, every tempted creature and every self-righteous Pharisee. He knows as certainly as each individual soul does, just what it feels like. He knows what it is to be crucified in us by sin, while all the time seeking to raise up to life again our consciousness of himself. "For this is life eternal, that they might know thee, the only true God, and Jesus Christ whom thou hast sent" to reveal him (John 17:3).

Is not this the stupendous and awe-inspiring revelation which was made by Jesus Christ? God manifest in the flesh. Every part of his incarnation, life as a man, and death on the cross—yes, and his glorious resurrection is a revelation of this truth. No wonder the apostles so loved to insist on the resurrection and seemed to make it the heart and center of their gospel! The real good news is the revelation of God conquering sin and bringing life to us, and working with transforming power in the hearts of those who have responded to the revelation made; and conscious of his life risen in us.

Yes, everything written concerning him in the Scriptures seems to confirm this truth. Everything that happened to him from his birth to his ascension had to happen. The Scriptures had to be fulfilled for they shadowed forth the full and perfect revelation of the real truth.

I used to be greatly puzzled when I read over and over again that the Lord Jesus deliberately did certain things, that the Scriptures might be revealed. In my blindness, it seemed to me that the prophecies ought to have been allowed to work themselves out instead of being, as it were, forced to happen. But, of course, the Savior had to make them happen and to act them forth, every one of them. He knew the truth and that all those old prophecies and the types and shadows of the Old Testament were all true and must now be fully demonstrated and acted out so that the truth might be revealed in all its fullness.

The prophecies were like little fragments and pieces of the truth which must now be fitted together to give the full picture. He did not do anything that the Scriptures might be fulfilled in order to prove that the predictions made by the prophets were true predictions, and to save the reputations of the prophets (as I used to suppose was his purpose). He did this in order to act out a

full and perfect picture of the real truth—
God conscious of what it is for us to be fallen
men, God suffering with us in our fall, God
bearing all sin and all its results down to the
very last detail, yes—and God raising us up
to the life he planned for us when he created
us.

"Is it nothing to you, all ye that pass by?
Behold and see if there be any sorrow like
unto my sorrow which is done unto me"
(Lam. 1:2).

Then I began to see another thing which
had been hidden from me, that though
every part of this truth is so clearly shadowed forth in the Old Testament, and typi-
fied in the sacrifices, and foretold by the
prophets, and then manifested forth in all
its fullness by Christ, we only understand it
gradually and in stages as we too grow in
understanding. It is not that the teaching in
the Bible is a gradually unfolding revelation,
but that we only come to understand it
gradually ourselves, just as a child's understanding gradually develops.

And so the Scriptures do give us these
three impressions of the truth so that we may
learn as we are able to bear it. First we do
recognize God as the Creator, the high and
lofty one inhabiting eternity, dwelling in
light, utterly holy, a burning and consuming
fire to which at first we do not dare to approach because we do not recognize him as
holy love.

But also there are the passages where the seers and prophets speak of him as the suffering one, just as Moses had done through the types and shadows of the Tabernacle and the sacrifices. But the Jewish people also found it overwhelmingly difficult to grasp the significance of a suffering God, of the Creator on a cross, just as they were so unable to understand the revelation of the presence of God actually dwelling in a tent of skins, and just as later they could not, and would not, believe he was present and incarnate in a human body.

And how significant certain mysterious things in the prophecies have now become. I never could understand, for example, why in Isaiah 53 the whole prophecy was written in the past tense as though it had already happened instead of looking forward in the future tense to its future fulfillment. Of course not, for that would not have been true. Isaiah was speaking of something that had already happened, although the full revelation of the truth was still for the future.

He was wounded and has been wounded for our transgressions all along. From the moment of the first sin it began to be true. "Surely he hath borne our griefs and carried our sorrows." "In all their afflictions he was afflicted" (Isa. 63:9). "Himself bear our diseases." "Surely he hath borne our griefs and carried our sorrows" (Isa. 53:4). "The Lamb of God who bears the sin of the world." All these well-known passages now take on a marvelous and overwhelming significance, and a host of other ones as well.

And oh, how unutterably glorious is the revelation made to us through the resurrection of our Lord Jesus and his ascension. Who can attempt to put it in words! Is not this the joy set before him which made our Creator and Savior and Redeemer and Lover, think it so infinitely worthwhile to endure the shame and to despise the cross, because of the rapture of being able through his cross (his cross which is our cross too, the cross of sin's agony and misery and torment) to raise up to newness of life, poor fallen mankind, individual by individual.

To me, this new conception of my God and Savior has had a most extraordinarily revolutionary and transforming effect, not only in my own personal response to this God and Savior himself, but also in my whole outlook and attitude towards other human beings. For now I see them in an absolutely new light.

Never again can I despise, or shrink from, or be indifferent to, a single individual that I meet. Never again can I think anyone uninteresting or hardly worth bothering about, or that there is no need to be patient with them nor to love them! For, you see, now in everyone I meet, I see someone in whom the eternal God and Redeemer is conscious of being on a cross, feeling and bearing all that they feel and bear as cross, difficult, cunning, lonely, miserable, tempted, despised and disliked individuals. He knows and feels with them all that they feel and all the consequences of their sin and the consequences of all the cruel sins done against them by others.

God who is of purer eyes than to look on evil without the utmost loathing and horror —yes, and hate—God unable to conceive himself—much less to bring into existence even a speck of evil—for love's sake refusing to become unconscious of fallen men and women. In some mysterious and awful sense, in all the men and women you and I meet: the fanatical, the narrow-minded and intolerant, the harsh and censorious, the perverted, the debased, the degraded, in little children whose innocence is deliberately destroyed, in the maimed and the twisted and the distorted, the despairing and the bestial, he has chosen to remain with all of us and to identify himself with us just as we are, at awful cost to himself, that he may bring to life in us again our lost consciousness of himself, and so save us.

And now to me new meaning has come into his last words and charge to the disciples. "Go ye into all the world and preach the gospel to every creature." This is the motive above all other motives, the one imperative motive to preach the gospel, to plead with men and women, to go to the uttermost ends of the earth—that our God and the Savior may be able to come down from his cross in them, as he has descended from his cross in us, and that he may see of the travail of his soul in them too and be satisfied. The missionary motive is not first and foremost to save them from hell, but that the Lamb of God who bears the sin of the world may descend from his cross and finish his glorious redemption.

Here too, at least as far as I can see, is the answer to the mystery of suffering, including the suffering even of little, innocent children. Love himself is in them, feeling it all, bearing it, crucified and rising to life making himself responsible to undo, in the end, all the results of sin, atoning for it (though how we still do not know), and bringing forth in his own good time resurrection life out of the agony and the death. It is all part of his cross. As Mother Julian once saw it, "We suffer with him on his cross."

Our fallen nature is his cross. Why it should be so we do not yet know, but we shall know one day, and now surely it is enough for us to know that in all our affliction he is afflicted, he bears our griefs and carries our sorrows, himself takes our diseases and bears our sicknesses. He identifies himself with us in utmost and complete reality.

Perhaps, in the light of this thought, there are some who will read the chapter on Christian unity again, with a clearer realization that it is indeed the suggestion of the great enemy of love, that we should separate from those we disagree with and should refuse to identify ourselves with them. For God our Savior is so identified with them that he is on a cross in them—waiting to come down and to begin his lovely and glorious work of raising them to life. And when we refuse to realize our oneness and to identify ourselves with all sinners, do we not nail our Lord afresh to the cross in our own lives?

How beautiful it is that the last book in the Bible closes with pictures of the victory of God's love and suffering and bearing. With what lovely new significance and awe and thankfulness and joy such passages as these break upon our understanding.

"After this I beheld, and lo! a great multitude whom no man could number, of all nations and kindreds and people and tongues, stood before the throne, and before the Lamb, clothed with white robes and palms in their hands; and cried with a loud voice saying, Salvation to our God who sitteth upon the throne and unto the lamb ... And they sang a new song saying ... thou art worthy ... for thou wast slain and hast redeemed us to God by thy blood out of every kindred and tongue and people and nation ... and every creature which is in heaven and on earth and under the earth, and such as are in the sea, and all that are in them, heard I saying, Blessing and honor and power and glory and power be unto him that sitteth upon the throne, and unto the Lamb for ever and ever."

You will want to read all of Hannah Hurnard's best-selling books.

Hinds' Feet on High Places. An allegory dramatizing the journey each of us must take before we can learn the secret of living life "in high places." Mass paper, a Living Book, $3.95.

Mountains of Spices. An allegory about human weaknesses and strengths, comparing the spices in Song of Solomon to the fruits of the Spirit. Mass paper, a Living Book, $3.50.

Hearing Heart. An autobiography. An intimate look into the life of Hannah Hurnard. Mass paper, $2.95.

Wayfarer in the Land. An epic of the author's experiences in bringing the Wayfarer's message to remote settlements in Israel. Mass paper, $3.50.

God's Transmitters. Prayer need not be a burdensome duty. It is meant to be a joyful and creative privilege. Mass paper, $2.95.

Walking Among the Unseen. A call to practice the New Testament pattern as the normal standard of life. Mass paper, $3.95.

Kingdom of Love. The ABC's of love presented here will enable us to represent God's love to those around us. Mass paper, $2.95.

Winged Life. This book presents five keys that will transform the way you think and make the "winged life" a reality. Mass paper, $3.50.

Hurnard 8-Volume Gift Set, $26.80